Hot Tea. . . Cold Case

a stephen blackman mystery

D.G. Stern

NEPTUNE PRESS

WWW.NEPTUNEPRESS.ORG

NEPTUNE PRESS

WWW.NEPTUNEPRESS.ORG

First Neptune Press edition: 2014
Printed in the U.S.A.

Publisher's Cataloging-In-Publication Data

Stern, D. G.
  Hot tea... cold case / D.G. Stern. -- First Neptune Press edition.

  pages ; cm. -- (A Stephen Blackman mystery)

  Originally published: Tiverton, RI : Yeoman House, c2007.
  ISBN: 978-0-9828098-2-2

  1. Scientists--Fiction. 2. Missing persons--Fiction. 3. Private investigators--Fiction. 4. Ebola virus disease--Fiction. 5. Suspense fiction. I. Title.

PS3619.T476 H68 2014
813/.6   2014947796

Life is too short to drink cheap wine.

CHAPTER ONE

I'm probably in the mood I'm in because of the weather. It sucks. Well, it's rather typical for a late fall New England day — gray, drizzly and forty degrees.

I might as well accept the fact that it's going to be one of those days. You know the kind I mean — when you feel sorry for yourself and begin to consider life in global terms. Not like peace in the Middle East or the price of gasoline type global, but more basic global. For example, why is it every time I read a detective novel, the hero has the body and sexual prowess of one of the Greek gods, the street smarts of an NYPD veteran, and the philosophical wisdom of a venerated rabbi? What about the basic fifty-year-old, slightly overweight, *I'll start the diet tomorrow type detective*? More food for thought: Why is every P.I. obsessed with weapons — something .45-caliber or 9-millimeter or 12-gauge? Consider the guy who not only doesn't own a gun, but who really doesn't like guns. I know this isn't something that will keep you up all night, but I am driven to consider all aspects of the human condition. It's probably something from my childhood. Sure, blame your mother when she's not around to defend herself.

One more question for consideration, since I'm on a roll. Why does every investigator's office look like the set from *The Maltese Falcon*, waiting for Bogie to walk in? What's wrong with an office in the local strip mall?

You are now, more likely than not, convinced that I've completely lost my mind and you'd be right…sort of. Let me introduce myself. I'm Stephen Blackman, a still-youthful fifty-something, Ivy League burned-out former lawyer, gun-hating detective who lives and works in an affluent suburb of Boston. I even mow my own lawn.

Early colonial history dictated most of New England's complex geography. The greater Boston area comprises four counties: Suffolk — which is Boston; Essex — generally to the north; Norfolk — generally to the south, except for the town of Brookline, which is in Norfolk County, but whose boundaries do not touch the boundaries of any other city or town in Norfolk County; and Middlesex County — generally to the west, where I reside.

Middlesex County is shaped like a dragon and covers an area from Cambridge all the way to the New Hampshire state line. Its borders were created in the eighteenth century by the dean of redistricting, Eldridge Gerry, from whose name comes the term *gerrymandering*. That concludes today's history lesson, although I think the fact that the same truths are evident today, and that selective redistricting is as prevalent as ever, says something about the last 200-plus years.

The town in which I live, Westham, like much of Middlesex County, is a post-World War II phenomenon. It lies between the more urban towns of Boston — Cambridge to the east and Worcester to the west. Although now almost extinct, working farms dominated the landscape well into the 1960s, when the building frenzy began to gobble up every inch of usable land. The situation has recently reached ridiculous heights...people buying perfectly good houses and tearing them down for the land, so they can build even bigger houses. Conspicuous consumption is reaching higher levels than I ever thought possible. It used to be that keeping up with the Joneses meant getting a new car every couple of years. Now it's getting a new house without getting rid of your current house.

You might well ask, what kind of work does a middle-aged suburban detective do? An excellent question and one that I contemplate on a daily basis. My stock answer is simple: I seek challenging cases that require a keen and resourceful mind. And is there enough of that kind of work to pay the mortgage on said house in that affluent suburb of Boston? Well...not exactly. It helps considerably that my kindly grandfather left me a modest inheritance, effectively eliminating the need to wrestle with whether to pay the electric bill or the gas bill.

Waiting for the phone to summon me hither or thither is akin to watching my beloved grass grow. I wonder if I should consider another career change — maybe write a book about my adventures as a detective. My computer monitor will only reflect my blank stare, since there is really nothing to write about yet. You see, I've had my P.I. license only about a month. I probably shouldn't contemplate a career change quite so soon. I'm really bummed out.

Like a clap of thunder, all this disgusting self-pity is at last interrupted by the incessant ringing of my phone. Bet it's a telemarketer.

"Blackman Investigations," I answer in my deepest baritone voice. "Steve? Ed Harris here."

Ed Harris is an acquaintance from my former life as a lawyer. He is a V.C., which too many men my age conjures up images of small men wearing black pajamas and carrying large guns through the jungle; but to everyone else it conjures up images of money, power, and bow ties. Ed is a venture capitalist, who invests about $300 million of other people's money in start-up companies, hoping to reap huge rewards when one of them goes public. As one might expect, Edwin T.J. Harris is pure prep: St. Paul's, Dartmouth, then a year off (good thing the draft was gone), followed by Harvard Business School. His club memberships include The Country Club (no kidding, that's its name); Somerset Club (dining on Beacon Hill overlooking Boston Common); Tennis and Racquet Club (the only club in Boston with a court tennis facility, which is not to be confused with ordinary tennis); and several others, plus the requisite community organizations. Despite all of this façade, Ed is bright, hard-working, and a genuinely nice guy — and there are so few these days.

The area upon which Ed focuses the investment portfolio of his clients is collectively known as *biotech*. Companies range from genetic engineering firms to manufacturers of soft tissue adhesion devices — Band-Aids.

"Hello Ed. To what do I owe the pleasure of this call?"

"I'm going to make your day." Ed doesn't sound a bit like Clint Eastwood.

"Well, it's about time somebody did."

"How are you holding up?" Ed's concern is genuine.

"There are good days and there are bad days."

"Then I guess you are available for an assignment. It is rather important to us. There is significant urgency to the problem."

"Let me check my schedule and see if I can squeeze you in," I reply. I can be really obnoxious without trying. "Yes, there's room. Shall we meet or shall we talk first?"

"Meet, and as soon as possible. Since you're free, so to

speak, my office tomorrow at ten o'clock. It'll take an hour or so to bring you up to speed, and then we can get a bite to eat."

"Any background I need?" I hope my thirst for a hint of what's in store for me isn't too obvious.

"Come at ten. And Steve, Henry is going to be sitting in on the meeting. Bye." The phone goes dead.

I stare at the handset. It must be important. The *Henry* to whom Ed referred is Henry Adams Barnett III, a wonderful, silver-haired gentleman of the old school, who earned his money the truly old-fashioned way — he inherited it. Not only did he inherit it, he made it grow through wise, well-researched investments. Now, people ask Henry's firm to invest money for them. However, they are usually disappointed — not with the results, but with the fact that Henry has closed the fund and simply will not accept any more money for investment. How truly sad. Not only did Henry close the fund, he has hired away many of the best people in the investment community to run the company, and Ed Harris is at the top of the heap. But a meeting that includes Henry? I am impressed.

Now I have additional pressing issues facing me — what to wear? Tweed sport coat or suit? Jeans and a Turtleneck is not even worth considering. Suit. It was my staple for twenty-five years, so why change? Because my entire life has changed, that's why. Compromise — gray flannel pants and a blue blazer. Can't go wrong.

The sun is even beginning to shine.

CHAPTER TWO

The morning begins as it did yesterday — gray, drizzly, and forty degrees. What keeps New Englanders going each day is the knowledge that if you wait around a few hours, the weather will change. I'm feeling a bit lightheaded. I may have my first detective assignment. Slow down, I tell myself. Don't get too excited. You haven't been hired yet. Don't count your chickens, etc. Remember, that's what got you in trouble way back when.

I have learned from painful experiences that it is best not to expect too much. If something good happens, then you will be twice as excited, but if nothing good happens, you'll only be half as disappointed. Sounds weird, but it works — at least for me.

Ed's offices or rather the offices of Capital Investments, are located, as one would expect, near the top of one of Boston's premier office buildings with, I might add, the worst parking.

As I head onto the *Mass. Pike*, colloquial for

6

the Massachusetts Turnpike (a fully paid-for toll road, the revenue from which is one of Massachusetts's biggest political footballs), I absent-mindedly throw four quarters into the awaiting toll basket. This is Boston's *ring road, which* encircles the Northeast's equivalent of Silicon Valley. Almost any computer-related company worthy of mention has an office on 128. The problem is that 128 is no longer the name of the road — something to do with interstate highway funds. The numeric designation of one of the most important and frequently traveled byways has been officially changed to I-93 or I-95, depending on where you are. Confused? When traveling in the Boston area, you had better know the name of the road on which you are driving, because only the cross streets have name signs, never the street you are on. I really must get one of those easy pass things, but that would be giving in.

I aim my trusty, rusty old Volvo, red in color to hide the hideous scars of New England winters, east toward the Financial District. The stretch of the Mass. Pike on which I am now traveling is affectionately known as the *extension*, since the transportation czars of forty years ago ended the Mass. Pike at Route 128, thus discouraging cars from driving into downtown Boston.

Another toll basket, four more quarters and I approach the infamous site of the former *Big Dig*. For those of you not familiar with Boston, the Big Dig was the biggest public works project in the country, designed to move more cars in and through Boston than the city could ever handle. Worse still, the design was obsolete before the first shovelful of dirt was moved. Construction disrupted everything, including ugly, cat-sized rats, which formerly resided in miles of underground pipes tunnels laid open by giant earthmovers.

Another tidbit for the uninformed traveler arriving in Boston, especially one driving a car: quarters. Always carry quarters. You need quarters for tolls, you need quarters for the phone, especially if you forgot to charge your cell phone, and most important, you need quarters for those rare metered parking spaces in downtown Boston.

Much like the one I have just found. I have a feeling that it's going to be a great day.

Alighting from the car, I stuff eight quarters into the meter, sufficient for only two hours. I make a mental note to feed the meter between my meeting and lunch, or else I will be greeted with a Day-Glo orange ticket for fifty dollars. Briefcase in hand, empty except for three yellow legal pads — old habits are hard to break, I enter the lobby of Zero Financial Plaza, an imposing high-rise office complex. I often wonder who the ornate atrium is intended to impress — surely not employees. Maybe *naïve* clients. I say naïve because each tenant is paying rent for a couple of square feet of this overdone, self- congratulatory symbol of the building's developer, which in turn gets passed on to the client in the form of increased fees.

I forget how much I loathe being in downtown Boston during the workday. I find myself nodding to a number of people who seem to recognize me or simply nod out of habit. I locate the correct elevator bank (as much by accident as intent), enter, and push the button for the forty-fourth floor.

The offices of Capital Investments are not at all what one expects. Although the forty-fourth floor has only one tenant, the elevator opens onto a corridor rather than the typical grand lobby replete with receptionists, expensive furnishings — you know, like a Hollywood version of a very expensive, high-rise office. Instead, I am facing a simple brass sign emblazoned with the words "Capital Investments, LLC" and an arrow pointing to the plain wooden door on the right. I twist the knob. The door is locked. I ring the bell next to the door. It buzzes back at me, and I enter. *Unfriendly.*

The reception area consists of a single, semi-circular desk, housing two efficient-looking, severe-looking women of uncertain age, except they would never see sixty again. The women are indistinguishable — twins? The balance of the smallish room contains four chairs: comfortable cloth living room-type chairs, not leather, not antique wingbacks, just plain, basic chairs. No magazines, no *Wall Street Journal* — nothing to read. Maybe I was supposed to bring my own. Although there are windows behind the reception desk, the floor plan discourages sightseeing.

Without looking up, Receptionist Number One says, "Mr. Blackman, you are expected."

How does she know who I am? I ponder. Creepy.

In less than a minute, a door to the left of the dynamic duo opens. I half expect Ed Harris's assistant, whom I envision as a beautiful, brainy recent graduate of The Business School, learning the ropes from the master. For those of you who are not versed in Boston snobbery, *The* Business School is Harvard Business School, and just like *The* Law School is Harvard Law School and *The* Medical School — you get the idea.

I don't disguise my surprise when Henry III enters. Almost diminutive (barely five feet five inches), he is very trim, walks erect despite his seventy-plus years, and wears a gray Brooks Brothers suit and a bow tie. Style can never be taught, it is instinctive.

Quickly he crosses the room and extends his hand to me. "Stephen, good to see you. Everyone is waiting."

"Everyone?" I say half-aloud.

"Ed has been joined by two members of the management team from Genetic Scientific Solutions. They're in the main conference room."

My first real hint of what is going on, albeit small.

Henry leads us through the door from which he entered. Tradition has it that the main conference room in any downtown Boston office tower, whether occupied by a corporation or a law firm, offers a spectacular view of the harbor. The décor always suggests something nautical: a binnacle, ship models, or just plain old original eighteenth-century paintings depicting vessels entering faraway ports, delivering goods from the mills of New England.

As we walk down the narrow and rather plain hallway, all I can see are doors, all closed. Next to each door is a plastic plaque bearing the name of the occupant and what appears to be a phone extension. The two words that pop into my mind are *sterile* and *efficient*. The work environment is an extension of the reception area.

We finally come to an intersection of corridors. Four large rooms face us. The two outside rooms are glass, each almost twenty by twenty feet. The two interior rooms are walled. Henry opens the door to the glass-walled room on the left. A sign announces *Employees' Lounge*.

The view is spectacular. As far as the eye can see. Just imagine what it would be like on a clear day — Boston Harbor all the way to Cape Cod. On a midsummer's day, scores of sailboats will display their sails below like sheets drying in the wind. I could never work under such ideal conditions. I'd spend the entire day dreaming about people and places far away.

While the employees may have little cubicles in which they labor, when they do take a break, the lounge is incomparable. The room is elegant and yet comfortable.

"Each Tuesday afternoon at four o'clock, Capital Investments has a staff meeting here." The boss beams with pride about *his* workplace. "Attendance, while urged, is not mandatory, although the turnout is usually 100 percent of those in the office. We discuss just about everything from investments to politics, from fashion to the Red Sox. If someone is troubled by something within the office environment, they are encouraged to speak — no holds barred and everything is off the record. Quite frankly, managing money can be very stressful, and this type of interaction seems to create an atmosphere in which everyone feels a level of empowerment. We are proud of the fact that we have very little turnover, and I attribute this, in part, to the candor expressed in these meetings and our willingness to listen and act."

I never expected this degree of social awareness from a bunch of money managers. I am pleasantly surprised.

"After the discussion portion of the meeting is concluded, we serve a catered dinner, with both wine and soft drinks. With few exceptions, namely an occasional child-related obligation or travel, everyone stays."

As we leave the conference room, Henry nods toward the other glass-walled room.

"And that's daycare. We have certified child care personnel, and any employee with a preschool child is encouraged to use the facility at no cost."

Wow, Henry really is socially conscious. Colorful drapes cover the glass, but shadows of little people bustling back and forth filter through.

We turn toward the walled room to the left. Henry opens the door. Other than a table at which ten could sit comfortably in matching chairs, the room looks like a NASA space center. Computer paraphernalia, monitors, keyboards, consoles, and printers all surround the conference table.

Houston, we've got a problem, is my immediate thought.

I'm sure my mouth is hanging open. Ed Harris rises from his chair and says, "Steve, I would like to introduce you to Kristen Marks, acting CEO of Genetic Scientific Solutions, Inc. and Robert Galjarian, managing director of Blue Water

Investors, who together with Capital Investors are the lead investors in GSS."

I once again become conscious of where I am.

Both Kristen and Robert rise as Ed is making introductions. We all exchange handshakes, reminding me of the coin toss before a football game when all the co-captains gather around the referee.

Kristen is as petite as Robert is large. She is as fair as he is dark. She is as attractive as he is — well, you know what I mean without me sounding politically incorrect. The contrast is startling, although I immediately have the sense of a shared purpose. Their ages are not easily ascertainable. Kristen looks younger than I think she is, and Robert older. I split the difference and put each of them in their mid-forties.

Kristen is wearing what I imagine to be the latest look for the professional acting CEO — a beige suit, ecru silk blouse, and a simple string of pearls, the real thing. Robert is wearing the basic power suit, although it looks rumpled. Not *slept-in* rumpled, but like the minute he put it on, it just — rumpled.

"I think Kristen should give a quick overview of what she's found at GSS during the last few weeks." Ed's curtness surprises me.

I am unaccustomed to remaining silent. "Would someone give me just a bit more background, like what does GSS do? Where are their offices? What is the corporate structure? I couldn't help but notice that Ms. Marks…"

"Kristen is fine," she says.

"…Kristen, is acting CEO, which is a somewhat novel title," I say.

"Good point." Henry leans forward. "Ed, I think some background might help put what we now know into perspective."

Ed is smiling. "Sorry, Steve, I forgot you've got no

idea what's going on."

So what else is new?

"Genetic Scientific Solutions, GSS to the world, was founded three years ago by two ex-Harvard Medical School employees with about $250,000 in seed money, presumably from family and friends." Ed crosses his hands. "The principals were both researchers but with no clinical experience, specializing in little-known cultures."

"Little-known cultures? Sounds like anthropology." I think I just put my foot in my mouth just trying to be clever based on the looks I am getting.

"To be more precise, they were conducting research in the identification and isolation of micro-organisms — primarily viruses. Many of these organisms had never before been isolated, so the distinction between unknown and new strains was blurred."

"Ed, if it's of any help, I began my college career in biochemistry, so I am at least marginally familiar with the basics." I am trying to figure out where this is all going.

"Right."

Henry, who is sitting in the back of the room, rises from his chair. "Let me take over for a minute."

Everyone stops talking.

"Stephen, you're here *because* of your background, not in spite of it. There are some preliminaries that need to be put in perspective. Two very bright young men, working on the cutting edge of science, combining theory, genetic engineering, empirical testing, and luck, isolated several organisms. These organisms demonstrate properties that might have huge economic potential. University research doesn't pay what the private sector does. The two scientists took their leave from Harvard and started up their own research and development company on a shoestring. Up to this point, nothing really amiss. People leave the university environment for start-ups all the time. And they take with them whatever it is they are working on. Our scientists made copies of their notes and didn't sabotage the experiments, which sometimes isn't the case. It is suspected that as the research began to develop more results, the notes became less copious, leaving our two scientists with unique knowledge to further develop their work. Once again, rather standard practice."

"So far so good." I just can't keep my mouth closed for any length of time.

"Their research continued, although the pace was slowed by their lack of proper laboratory facilities. Remember, the quid pro quo for many university scientists is the opportunity to use state-of-the-art equipment, surrounded by colleagues who are among the best and the brightest."

"Enter venture capital," Ed interjects with a smile, which immediately leaves his face under a stony glare from Henry. This is Henry's show until he relinquishes the floor.

"Since we are moving closer to the present," Henry continues, "I will start adding names and dates. I suggest that note-taking is in order."

Immediately, everyone grabs a pen and a pad, even though I suspect that with the exception of myself, these facts have long since been committed to memory by the balance of the assembled group.

"Lazlo Frederick Onellon, scientist number one. Born in Pittsburgh. Parents were Hungarian refugees. Graduated from Stanford majoring in mathematics, then received a Ph.D. with distinction from U. Cal Berkeley in biology. There is no explanation for the change of academic direction. He completed his post-doctoral work at Columbia in the area of genetics. He then continued his research at The Medical School working on a project to genetically engineer vaccines for several rather nasty diseases. Onellon was later joined at

Harvard by Theodore Gordon, who graduated from Johns Hopkins at age nineteen and received his Ph.D. in chemistry from MIT. After Gordon joined Onellon, they became as one, working until all hours, sometimes all night. Although they bonded almost immediately, there was never a suggestion that the relationship extended beyond two extremely talented and driven scientists working on a project that possessed them.

"For over a year and a half, the two struggled with their research, producing few results. The team was becoming depressed, and continued funding was becoming questionable. Onellon and Gordon received an invitation to attend a seminar in Tel Aviv, featuring some of the world's most renowned genetic scientists. What they came away with from the seminar is not at all clear, except that upon their return, the entire direction of the research changed. Experiments began yielding results. The mood at the lab improved, and everyone was upbeat. Suddenly, the pair left The Medical School."

Henry does not even take a breath. "Would anyone like coffee or tea?"

The break will give me a chance to absorb the monologue.

I take the opportunity not to only make myself a cup of tea (I have a four-cup-a-day Earl Grey habit), but to see if I can chat for a few minutes with Kristen and Robert, basically, Kristen.

Since *What is a nice girl like you doing in a place like this?* is a really lame line, I decide to try "Hi, would you like some sugar for your coffee?" proffering the sugar bowl.

"Thanks, but I drink mine black." Robert rolls his eyes. I can't tell if I'm interrupting something or Robert just isn't a tea drinker.

"Thank you." The beautiful acting CEO, with a knockout smile, takes two packets from the sugar bowl, which visibly trembles in my outstretched hand. "Coffee needs to be sweet."

My heart stops.

I seize the opportunity to further engage the already-engaging acting CEO in meaningful dialogue. "How is it you got the job at GSS?"

"It's what I do." Her smile is deadly. "For about three years, I have acted as a kind of traveling troubleshooter." All I can think of is the calling card of Richard Boone: Have Gun, Will Travel. Kristen's card probably reads, ***Have Briefcase, Will Travel.***

"Let's get started again," returns me to reality.

I forget how much I hate reality.

CHAPTER THREE

Everyone quickly returns to the table. No one attempts musical chairs. We are all back in class, and the professor is resuming the lecture.

"GSS was founded shortly thereafter, a little less than two years ago, by two brilliant men doing research in an area about which little is really known. They scraped together a few dollars, the source of which may turn out to be less certain than originally thought. They found a new sense of purpose, direction, and enthusiasm. What next? More money. But how do two biotech scientists with an idea get money? Simple: Find someone who can prepare a business plan and hand it out on a street corner in Kendall Square; by the end of the day, you would probably have a million dollars." Henry looks at his captive audience for its approval of his attempted humor.

For those of you who wonder what Henry is talking about, let me translate. Before the bubble burst, businesses in research and development in the field of genetics, like their e-commerce brothers, could raise money almost without trying.

Kendall Square is an area in Cambridge, across the Charles River from Boston, where MIT-types and those whose work is of a scientific/high-tech nature, hang out. Modern buildings have replaced most of the traditional brick warehouses in which some of the world's best minds have discovered, invented, and otherwise created everything from indestructible fabrics to electric cars — from lasers to audio speakers.

Two researchers with the credentials of Lazlo and Theodore would have had no trouble raising money for their experiments, but that was then.

"In what seemed like a logical move, Onellon and Gordon recruited the help of a young Sloan School graduate to help prepare a business plan." Henry looks around the table.

Despite what many people think, MIT is home to one of the top business schools in the country, the Sloan School, although they work hard to keep it a secret.

"Jacob Kettleman is an Israeli, who holds degrees in both engineering and physics from the University of Tel Aviv, as well as having graduated with high honors from Sloan," Henry continues. "He appears to be in his mid-thirties, but his previous employment history is somewhat obscure. That comes later. Kettleman seems to have had some direct connection to Onellon and Gordon, possibly through the seminar they attended in Israel. Anyway, the three of them got together and prepared what quite candidly is the best, clearest, and simplest business plan I have ever read. Ever!"

That is probably the most emphatic expression ever uttered by our host, but it must be true, since both Ed and Robert simultaneously nod in agreement.

"I'm sorry to interrupt, Henry, but why all the cloak-and-dagger stuff? This has to do with your investment in GSS, doesn't it?" So why am I beginning to feel so uncomfortable?

"Yes and no." Kristen adds.

"Yes and no?" I hate it when I am treated as though I am clueless, regardless of whether I am or not.

"Stephen," Henry continues purposefully. His eyes narrow as he speaks. "This has got to do with a lot more than a mere investment. While I appreciate your eagerness to get to the bottom of the story, things are not what they seem. I do promise that when I have completed my presentation, everything will fit together nicely."

I have the uncanny ability to stick my foot directly into my mouth. Why can't I learn to keep my thoughts to myself for at least a minute or so?

"Apparently, the business plan was sent directly to six different investor groups," Henry continues. "How these groups were targeted is unknown, except that each firm is private, low-key, and quite successful." Henry nods to Robert, who ever so slightly nods back.

"Normally, unsolicited business plans are given only a quick review. This plan, however, was extraordinary."

"Henry..." Robert Galjarian stands to address the group. "It occurs to me that unlike a lot of venture firms, those to whom the plan had been sent have at least one thing in common: every business plan submitted to our firms is read at least once.

"Because of the nature of their proposal, I suggest they were supremely confident that our interest in GSS would be piqued, and indeed they proved correct," Robert continues.

I scratch my head. "You seem certain that only six plans were sent out."

"They were numbered one of six, two of six, et cetera,"

Robert says.

Why do I insist on making myself appear stupid?

"Good point." Henry resumes control. "Good point. Where was I? Oh yes. At least in our shop, the plan was immediately recognized for its quality and sent to Ed for his attention. He, in turn, gave it to me. Within a week, we scheduled an interview with the management team of Onellon, Gordon, and Kettleman."

"Henry, I know I'm being impatient," I say. "Considering that everyone else, except me, has read this tome, pray tell what was this extraordinary trio trying to sell? They seem to have convinced several high-powered venture firms to give them money."

"If you had a chance to invest in a cure for cancer, would you do so?" Before I can answer, Henry continues. "Technically, a vaccine to prevent most forms of cancer? Simply said, that is what they were trying to sell."

"Isn't that just a bit far-fetched? A vaccine that would actually prevent cancer."

"Not if the cause for cancer is isolated and a vaccine genetically engineered to attack the cause." Kristen speaks for the first time. "Imagine the cause of measles being identified and then isolated. A preventative vaccine could be formulated."

"But that's been done!" I am showing off my limited knowledge.

"Exactly." Kristen pauses. "Why not cancer, provided you can identify and isolate the cause?"

"Okay, I'll shut up. If these guys are on the right track, why are you so worried about your investment?"

"Stephen, I've asked for your patience, because this is a little more complicated than it appears on the surface." Henry begins to pace. "To be brief, each of the six venture firms elected to invest. GSS was only seeking a total of 8 million dollars, of which Capital and Blue Water invested 2.5 million each, with the balance being divided amongst the remaining four investment groups. Round one. Each firm elected one director to the board to serve with the founders. They never sought control, which is refreshing, to say the least, although they did retain almost 60 percent of the stock ownership."

I am totally confused. How else can one be confused, other than totally? I'm really slipping away.

"Ed..." Henry tries to stifle a yawn. "Please describe to Stephen a quick overview of the first year's activities, while I excuse myself for a minute."

Ed starts to rise, as if to deliver a lecture, but sensing that he is being passed the baton only for a little while, decides to remain seated.

"So?" I look at Ed.

"Everything was perfect. We received weekly written status reports, biweekly conference calls, and had monthly board meetings, together with financial statements showing how every penny had been spent. From time to time, either Robert or I, would get calls from Kettleman asking our advice on financial matters, like should they lease rather than purchase a piece of equipment, should they accelerate depreciation, that sort of stuff. These guys were running a start-up from heaven. They continually compared where they were in terms of research ho the timeline they set out in the business plan, and if they didn't exceed expectations, which they consistently did, they provided us with a detailed explanation."

"Sometimes too detailed," Robert adds.

Ed nods in agreement. "They seemed really upset that they had somehow failed us."

"It was too good to be true," Robert says. "We've been in probably forty or fifty deals, and we were never given information so freely and completely. At one point, we got suspicious and sent our accountants in for a surprise audit. I expected that these guys would raise the roof, but instead, we were greeted like long-lost relatives, especially by Kettleman, who spent days going over every entry with the accountants. I finally had to recall the accounting team, for fear that the cost of this surprise audit might run into tens of thousands of dollars. Bottom line, the bean counters reported that this was the best set of books they had ever seen. Ed and I then discussed whether we should hire an outside tech type to review the science. We asked several of the other investors, whom we had told about the audit. The consensus was that we would be wasting money and possibly offending Onellon and Gordon, who were working about twenty-four hours a day, basically trying to make us money. In hindsight I'm not sure the decision was correct, although it probably wouldn't have made any difference."

"Any difference to what?" I'm almost shouting.

Henry speaks in a soothing voice as he re-enters the the room. "Remember that I said this was complicated."

I acknowledge by nodding.

"We're now almost up to date. Please be patient. Ed, I'll finish up."

"It appears that GSS was progressing in accordance with its business plan. We were all pleased. About eight months ago, we received a call from Kettleman. He was extremely agitated. His original financial forecasts had a burn rate that would take the company through the FDA approval process, but it now seemed that certain tests that were being conducted would require somewhat more time than originally forecasted to complete. He was really quite upset. Kettleman asked, actually demanded, that a board meeting be scheduled for the following week.

"All the directors appeared in person. We have all

been through this process many times before with other investments — the baleful cry for more money. With 8 million invested, which we thought had been a little on the low side initially, I think we were all prepared for the worst. Those in attendance, including both Ed and myself on behalf of Capital, were given a complete package, including detailed financials. The meeting started with both Onellon and Gordon explaining the problems with the trials, the size of the study — basic technical issues that confront almost every company seeking product approval. Kettleman next began a detailed slide presentation of the financials. After about ten minutes, I interrupted Kettleman and asked him how much he was seeking in additional funding. Sheepishly he said, *about eighty thousand dollars.* Everyone in the room gasped with relief. We had all assumed that the overrun would be at least a million and a half dollars. GSS had just put on a multimillion-dollar presentation for a 1 percent increase in funding. By noon the next day, each investor group had wired in its pro rata share."

I just can't contain myself. "It's been over an hour and all I know is that these guys are Boy Scouts. Since Kristen is here and since I'm here, there must be a punch line."

"You've endured a lot, and the end is near. The next six months progressed flawlessly: reports, conference calls and meetings. Three weeks ago last Monday, the Commonwealth of Massachusetts celebrated Columbus Day. GSS was closed for the holiday, or so it seemed."

I'm listening, but I'm not understanding.

"On the Tuesday following Columbus Day, Onellon, Gordon, and Kettleman failed to show up for work. No one could remember when one of them, much less all three, had ever missed a day of work. Then the real problems became apparent. The hard drives on their personal computers had been removed, and all backup discs and both Onellon's and Gordon's research notes were gone. All accounting and administrative functions were untouched. No money had been taken out of the corporate accounts. It's as if any evidence of Onellon, Gordon, and Kettleman ceased to exist. Needless to say, without the science, GSS is basically worthless."

It takes a second for me to absorb all this.

"By five o'clock that afternoon, we decided to hold a telephonic board meeting and agreed to keep everything under wraps until we could figure out what was going on. Kristen was recommended as someone who could assume immediate control, while a game plan was being formulated. You, Stephen, are now part of the game plan."

I think I was just paid a compliment. Why do I get the sense that I am about to be thrown into a lion's den? Looking around the table doesn't make me feel any better.

Suddenly a phone rings and in almost perfect unison everyone reaches for their personal cell phones.

"Hello," Robert bellows. "Can't talk now. I'll call you when I can. I know it's important. I'm on top of it." He snaps the phone closed and places into his pocket without comment.

CHAPTER FOUR

I raise my hand, seeking permission to speak. Henry points at me, reminding me of my first-grade teacher. "Any word from the missing triumvirate?"

Henry shakes his head. "Nothing."

"Anything from any third party, someone making a demand, like kidnappers or terrorists — anyone?"

Once again Henry shakes his head.

"How about friends or family?"

You can hear a pin drop in this crowd.

"Absolutely nothing," Ed says.

I feel that first bead of cold sweat trickle down my back.

"Without acting too concerned or drawing too much attention to the situation, we've been able to ascertain that each of the three was home over the Columbus Day weekend at one time or another, but nothing more specific." Robert drums his fingers on the table. "They're very private people and no one was paying any attention to their comings and goings."

"It's been over three weeks, and whatever pieces of the puzzle still remain undiscovered will be virtually impossible to put together." I am talking to no one in particular, but trying to sound very detective-like. "I can't believe that there is nothing left of your 8 million dollar investment." I can't make eye contact with Henry, Ed, and Robert. They are all looking at the floor.

"There is no way to replicate the research without Lazlo and Theodore." Kristen speaks so quietly that we are forced to lean forward to hear her. "Even the work in progress is meaningless without their lab notes. Every bit of data was stored in their computers, using an elaborate encryption system they had developed. They were very concerned about security."

"What about Kettleman?" I say. "You said that all the financial material is intact. How does he fit into the disappearance?"

"Good question. We simply do not know." Robert contributes little new information. "The financial component of the company is as it should be, although whatever he had on his PC is gone."

"I guess my job, if I accept the assignment, will be to find the missing threesome and their research data. Is that correct?" I hope I am not being too simplistic.

"There's more." Henry slowly turns toward me.

"Good or bad?" I ask.

"Bad. It's extremely bad. In addition to their work on creating a vaccine for cancer, Onellon and Gordon were expanding their research to include vaccines for several other diseases…" Henry takes a deep breath. "They theorized that if you isolate and identity the cause of any disease, you can engineer a vaccine to protect someone from its effects. The fear of deadly and mysterious diseases is becoming a national preoccupation and not without reason, I might add. GSS built a special laboratory in which highly contagious diseases are being studied. This room is quite separate and apart from the general lab area, and special ventilation and other safety precautions have been installed. Anyone entering the room needs to wear protective clothing — almost like a space suit. One of the diseases they were examining was a very nasty strain of Ebola."

"Henry!" I'm sure my face is red, because I know I'm screaming. "That's the kind of disease that makes your skin shrivel so you end up like a mummy."

"Please don't jump to conclusions. There are scores of facilities throughout the United States working on solutions to biohazard issues. The nature of our work made us an ideal choice for disease research."

"Where's this going?"

"The disease laboratory has a time clock, so we know it was entered about six o'clock Monday morning, Columbus Day."

"And...?"

"And we don't know."

"Don't know what?"

"We don't know what was in the room."

"What do you mean you don't know what was in the room? There's got to be some kind of inventory or something — right?"

"Presumably so, but since only Onellon and Gordon are permitted access to the laboratory, whatever it was they were working on is..."

"   in their computers."

Henry nods, acknowledging my comment by closing his eyes, but only for a moment. "Yes, that's the problem. We have no idea what, if anything, is gone."

"That's outrageous!" I scream at anyone who is listening. "So for three weeks, all of you have been aware that this horrible stuff might be missing and have done nothing about it. This is an outrage by any standards!"

"We didn't have the slightest notion that the *stuff*, as you call it, might be missing until yesterday when Ed called you. All I can say with any certainty is that the secured lab was entered on Columbus Day."

"Could they have given the access code to someone else? Maybe under extreme duress." I don't have a good feeling about this.

"We don't know anything else, and I'm not going to push the panic button until I know more. That's what we want from you — information." Henry looks at each of us at the table, one by one.

"Come on. Only two people have authorized access to the lab from hell and they're gone. I don't understand why during the three weeks you decided to keep this under wraps, a thorough search of GSS hasn't been conducted." I'm sure I sound pissed…and scared.

"Stephen…" It's Kristen, trying to put on her sweetest and sexiest voice. "Everyone was looking the other way, at the cancer vaccine, not at the biohazard research."

"Makes sense. Look where the money is."

"Maybe in hindsight we could have handled everything differently, but that's not relevant to today. We want to retain your services so each and every aspect of the situation can be reviewed and a comprehensive strategy developed."

"Easier said than done." I squirm in my chair. "Hasn't it occurred to any of you that it is better to err on the side of caution, especially when there may be a killer virus out there? Jesus, we're talking about a potential catastrophe here."

Henry closes his eyes until only a slit remains and he

appears to be looking right through me. I'm not sure if he is upset at the situation or my language, probably both.

I stop to listen to myself. I am sounding, in no particular order, immature, unprofessional and scared. What I need is to be calm, cool and collected and scared. Fear is sometimes a very good thing. I find it incomprehensible that it took three weeks to figure out that someone entered the secured laboratory. I take a deep breath. Since no one knows what, if anything was in the secured room, we can't know if anything was removed. So what's the big deal? Like a bolt of lightning, thoughts of bioterrorism and weapons of mass destruction flash through my mind. The stakes are so high — maybe too high. Like over-my-head high.

"I'm on board, but conditionally. I call it like I see it. Agreed?" I'm trying to remain totally professional, more or less. It's hard not to show emotion when the fate of civilization as we know it might be threatened.

I readily admit that I'm waffling whether to accept this assignment. If I'm so sure the plague or whatever is really gone, then as a reasonably sane person, I should be out of here in the next ten seconds. However, without a little more to go on, we might start a panic of unparalleled magnitude. I need to put everything in context. If GSS found out only yesterday that there might have been a security breach, and during the three weeks since the scientists' disappearance there've been no demands, maybe the situation isn't all that hopeless. I'd better stop trying to talk myself into this job before it's too late. Kristen is smiling. It's too late.

"Agreed," Henry announces, bringing me sharply back to reality, "except that you need to keep us in the loop daily. The ultimate decisions rest with you. Shall we discuss compensation?"

"Shit!" I jump up. "I've got to put some quarters in the meter."

Henry smiles. "My secretary will take care of it. Where did you park?"

CHAPTER FIVE

"What do you really know about the three missing men?" I look directly at Henry. "I mean, really know."

"Ed, please turn on the overhead," Henry says.

The room is immediately transformed from a benign conference room into a twenty-first-century information control center. Simultaneously, several dormant computer monitors come to life, and a screen silently drops from the ceiling, while a projector casts its beacon toward the far wall. The overhead projector is hooked up to a computer so that the image on the monitor can be enlarged onto the wall screen. Not only can we see a single image from a single computer, but the device can split the screen so that we are able to view three different monitors at the same time. So much for home movies.

Henry walks toward a console that appears to have been designed by the joint efforts of Bill Gates and George Lucas. He picks up a laser pointer and with a simple nod of his head, the production begins as the lights dim and three faces appear on the screen. I silently yearn for popcorn.

The first picture is of a man — late thirties, bearded, short red hair, mandatory wire-rim glasses, a turtleneck sweater showing around the edges of the beard — in short, a typical science nerd.

The red light points at the face reminding me of movies where the bad guys sometimes the good guys — aim laser-sighted weapons at their intended victims an instant before…pow!

"Lazlo Onellon," Henry lectures.

No surprise there.

The next image is of a kid straight out of *Leave it to Beaver* — clean-shaven, probably never-shaven, nice smile showing a lot of teeth, neatly combed hair. I can envision his mother sitting near him, saying, *Smile for the nice man, Theodore.* Clearly I am looking at Gordon's yearbook picture.

Once again the red beam falls on the screen.

"Theodore Gordon."

Two out of three. Bet I guess the third.

A thin, angular portrait appears, dominated by a pair of dark, penetrating eyes. Looking at the face of Jacob Kettleman makes me very uncomfortable. There is definitely something creepy about this guy, but I can't quite figure it out. His look is not Middle Eastern, although he is an Israeli. I'm lost in thought, which is a nice way to say daydreaming because I awake to see Ed standing at my side.

Handing me a file folder, Ed explains, "Everything you need to know about these three men is in here, including various photographs, names and addresses of family and friends."

"Everything I need to know?"

"I'm sorry. I mean to say, it's all we've been able to pull together for you in such a short time. Consider it a starting point — a baseline."

"Well, I guess this is everything…" I wave the folder, "…except where they are."

Ed looks as if he has aged about ten years during the last two hours. I guess when you are dealing with a plague, there is little to feel good about. I still have this nagging feeling that something is missing. Why didn't the GSS team notify the proper authorities immediately and let them handle it? It's what they do. Is the missing or not-missing Ebola the issue or a red herring? Am I being used to buy time? From whom? Why? Or do they think I can bring order to this chaos — and why me? My head is spinning, and I want to throw up, thinking that a vial of Ebola is in the hands of some nutcase.

Henry again rises from his seat. "By and large, these dossiers are very straightforward, except for two minor anomalies."

How does he know about dossiers? Too many flicks, or is he a CIA operative? One look at Henry tells me the answer. Too many old movies.

"First, the seed money for GSS, which we were told had come from family and friends. We've been able to trace the source of the wire deposit to a numbered Swiss account."

This is looking worse and worse, I think.

"Secondly, and probably what makes the wire even more disturbing, is the fact that before Kettleman came to the U.S. to attend the Sloan School, he was in the Israeli army."

I roll my eyes. If this weren't so serious, I'd ask *what else?*

"Not only was he in the army," Henry replies to my thoughts, "but he was assigned to an intelligence unit."

He's a bright guy. Why give him a gun and send him into the desert? Intelligence is probably where he belonged. Next, Henry will tell me Kettleman is a Mossad agent.

"Needless to say, his leadership and intellectual

qualities were noticed immediately by his superiors and he spent the next six years attached to the Mossad."

"No shit," I mutter. No one is paying any attention to me.

Consider that following the seminar Onellon and Gordon attended in Tel Aviv, where Kettleman had served in an elite intelligence unit, their research was revitalized; the now-infamous business plan was developed by Kettleman; and the Swiss account. Now the sudden disappearance of the two scientists, their notes, and possibly one of the world's most deadly substances. I think I have every reason to be concerned.

I consult my ever-faithful plastic Swatch watch. "I, for one, need a little food, although I can understand if no else feels the same. I have a splitting headache and could really use something to eat." I suspect that I'm suffering as much from a lack of food as from the thought of the incredibly difficult task I've agreed to undertake.

Everyone is relieved with my great suggestion. Possibly Henry's story is getting to them as well. I don't think I can handle Chinese. Sandwiches from the *Hole in the Wall* deli will have to suffice.

CHAPTER SIX

Some people get excited about fabulous business plans. I get really turned on by a great ham and cheese with just a touch of Dijon on an onion roll. I'm glad the others decide to order lunch. I hate eating alone, although I have been getting used to it. Eating is supposed to be an experience, not simply an opportunity to stuff food in your face.

It does the soul good to take a few minutes and distance yourself from thoughts of apocalyptic viruses and missing scientists. The sandwich was outstanding. It is painfully clear that my new undertaking will be extremely difficult, if not impossible. I am expected to locate and return the missing *goods*. What if they have been forcibly taken? What can I deduce from the fact that there has been no communication from the abductors? Or is it possible that no one is telling me that there's actually been some kind of demand? Why would anyone go to all this trouble if they didn't want something? But what? The answer could be as unsettling as the question.

Classic reasoning is required. What's the motive? Depends on the perpetrators. There are three missing people, two of whom are critical in the research process. Was the Ebola an afterthought or the main target? If the latter, why bother with the scientists and their data? Or was it a ruse to divert our attention? From what? Where?

I can't answer either why or who. How? Less difficult to figure out, but also less relevant. When? I'm reasonably confident it's been narrowed down to the twenty-four-hour period from noon on Sunday to noon on Columbus Day. Where? Either from their homes, the office, or both. I don't think it really makes much difference. Put this all together and you've got one frustrated detective. It's like doing the *New York Times* crossword puzzle, but nothing is connecting. Corporate espionage or terrorism? The first is not good, the second is unthinkable, except that we had better give it some serious consideration.

"Stephen?" Henry picks up a napkin and wipes his hands. "Are you all right?"

I'm mumbling to myself again and I look up, suddenly aware that four pairs of eyes are staring at me. Oops.

"Sorry." I resist getting up and writing on the chalkboard. "I am trying to figure out a starting place. Can anyone suggest a motive?"

Robert raises his voice. "Seems rather obvious to me." I look at him with one eyebrow raised and the other lowered — a trick that I have been working on for years. "The motive is obviously the vaccine. It has almost limitless economic potential."

"It may also save a good many lives," Kristen adds.

"Then what about the Ebola?" The thought of Ebola, even in a safe environment, gives me goose bumps.

Henry and Ed nod thoughtfully.

"We are getting off the track," Robert asserts. "We

don't even know if it's gone, or was there in the first place... and if it is gone, it's probably a decoy. Any terrorist would have made a demand by now."

"A decoy? What if the Ebola was the goal and the kidnapping is a decoy? If we are dealing with a sophisticated terrorist organization, they may very well adopt a wait-and-see attitude." Once again I feel I am almost shouting.

"This is a fruitless argument. We know what is gone, why speculate on what might be gone?" Robert aggressively replies. "When you find any one of the three men, we'll know what's still missing...if anything. It really doesn't make a difference at this point."

I appreciate his vote of confidence, but...

"I agree," Kristen says.

Their logic assumes that if one finds the kidnapped scientists, the Ebola mystery will be solved. True, but that misses the point completely.

"Difference! Of course it makes a huge difference." I stop and slowly take a drink of water...buying time to think. I'm not sold on the idea that none of the other four people in this room is as clueless as I am. "Like life and death. Maybe we can't do anything about it, but it makes a big difference. If I conclude that Ebola has been removed from GSS, I'm on my way home. It becomes a new ball game and I'm not equipped to play. If the Ebola isn't missing, maybe the three men decided to take an unannounced sabbatical. If the Ebola is gone, the disappearance is undoubtedly connected. People who remove Ebola from an otherwise safe place are probably, quite likely — crazy, fanatical, and dangerous beyond belief, and there won't be any rules. I am only willing to listen because I believe you really don't know what's missing, however, I am still not convinced we shouldn't bring in the big guns."

"Stephen..." Henry's voice is soothing, but clearly concerned. Kristen, on the other hand, was taking my comments personally. "There is another problem."

"Locusts?" I am beginning to lose it.

"Apparently, in order to possess, much less experiment with, potentially harmful substances, permission is required from several state and federal agencies."

"Hurray," I think aloud. Maybe a thief will register with the local disease control agency. Then they can go and ask him for the Ebola. I am sure that it will be returned. I'm so far off track, that I never expected Henry's next statement.

"We have no record that GSS ever requested proper permission for the Ebola research. Now it might be …"

"…on the missing computers." I rub my forehead, trying to ward off a headache. "So the whole operation might be illegal as well?"

Henry barely moves his head.

"Illegal isn't the label I want to put on this." Kristen glares directly at me.

Maybe she will never forgive my outburst. *Love lost …once again.*

"Or it might mean there never was any Ebola and consequently no permission is needed." Robert's face turns red.

Good theory, but it doesn't wash.

Ed abruptly stands up and places the palms of his hands flat on the table. "Steve, we have had our attorneys research the various applicable statutes and regulations concerning the storage and care of material like Ebola. Failure to comply with the requirements gives rise to severe penalties."

Talk to the suits first. This explains the delay.

"Are the penalties more severe than being kidnapped or having a national epidemic?"

"Depends on whose point of view." Kristen bites her lip.

I am dumbstruck. I turn toward Henry. "What is your point of view?"

He clears his throat. "Besides huge fines, for which the directors of the corporation may be personally liable, criminal sanctions are virtually mandated and the directors, at least those who haven't disappeared, may be prosecuted. I can envision certain elements of the law enforcement community trying to make names for themselves, as well as setting an example, all in the name of anti-terrorism. Stephen, we could be opening a Pandora's Box...for nothing. This matter requires speed, efficiency and discretion. "

"Henry..." My voice is cracking. "Speed, efficiency, and discretion require an army of trained professionals. It's the kind of thing the FBI does every day. I've got no real leads, and three critical weeks have been lost. And don't forget that a bottle of death may be out there somewhere, with the world's clock ticking away. Whoever is involved could be anywhere in the world. And if the connection between GSS, Kettleman, and Mossad is more than coincidental, we are in the big league...I mean the really big league. Way, way over my head."

"If you don't think you can handle it." Robert sneers at me.

"That's exactly what I am saying. This may be too big for anyone, and we have no place to start. Thanks for the confidence, Henry, Ed, if there's nothing else I know, it's when to stop. It was a hard lesson, but I at least learned it." I start to rise.

"Please sit down!" Henry slaps the table with the palm of his hand. "One week. That is all I want from you. Do what you do. Look, read, talk, analyze, and come back in one week with a recommendation. We will give you as much support as you think you need. For starters, Kristen will be working with you vis-à-vis background material and access.

Whatever you need. You will be compensated at $350 per hour plus all expenses."

I am tempted to say that in one week I will undoubtedly suggest that contacting the FBI is mandated, unless some idiot unleashes an Ebola horror before then. If we wait a week, I could be jeopardizing my license, obstructing justice, or something even worse. Why am I wasting another minute thinking about this? I look around the room. Kristen is smiling. Is the ice princess thawing? Or I am just projecting? The fee is rich, too rich for a detective, but strangely comparable with the going rate for legal fees. What can I accomplish in a week? A year for that matter? I guess that means I can park in a parking lot. Shit...my meter is about to expire. I look at my watch.

"Since nothing has happened in the last three weeks, before I commit to the engagement, I want to poke around — say forty-eight hours of preliminary review, and then another meeting. Okay?" I presume the nods around the table indicate a consensus. I am going to regret this, I'm sure.

"I'm not being mercenary, but who is hiring me?"

"GSS." Robert's reply is immediate.

"Another two days might allow me to organize this mess for the big guys to take over, which I see as inevitable." Sometimes working from the inside out, rather than the outside in, allows information to flow more quickly and with a less defensive spin.

I hear a collective sigh from those assembled. I'm positive that somebody or maybe everybody isn't telling me everything I should know. But why?

"Where shall we begin?" I direct my gaze at Kristen.

"Let's try the beginning." Is she being cute or what? "I think you should take a minute or two and review the dossier."

I heft the document. Lawyers always seem to charge

by the pound for paperwork. This is going to take more than a few minutes.

Henry turns to me. "Have you ever considered using a credit card in the smart parking meter?"

CHAPTER SEVEN

It isn't until my stomach starts growling that I realize how absorbed I've been in reading the files. A quick look at my watch tells me almost three hours has passed, during which time Ed, Henry, and Robert have fled, quietly, I might add. Only the faithful Kristen has kept me company, although I was unaware of her presence. Big-time social failure. A beautiful woman alone in a conference room and I ignore her. Well, I am working. So is she, because when I finally look up, she is deep into note-taking. The material I've been examining is thorough and in-depth. I wonder how much of the information had been prepared prior to Capital's investment in GSS and how much has been assembled since the present crisis? I shudder when I consider what kind of dossier they have on me. Scary! I really need a cup of tea. I feign a yawn, which I accompany with the prerequisite stretch, immediately getting Kristen's attention.

"Think we can get room service?" Am I being too

suggestive or simply clever?

"Earl Grey — black. And you're forgiven. Calling the research illegal was a bit much, but it did get everyone's attention."

"And a coffee with two sugars."

The words are no sooner out of our mouths when in walks Ed. "Time for a break?"

Since I'm suspicious by nature, I look around to see if there are any concealed cameras that have been spying on us. I don't even want to think about it. This case really is beginning to resemble *Mission: Impossible*.

Ed quickly moves to the phone and asks for a tray of beverages and light refreshments. He actually says: *beverages and light refreshments*. Maybe there *is* room service. As I stand up, I realize how stiff I am and how isolated I feel. For the last six hours, I have been literally holed up in a windowless room. Is it day or night outside? Is it raining or clear? And does it really make any difference in light of the fact that there may be some fruitcake out there with a bottle of Ebola? My wandering thoughts are interrupted by a knock on the door.

A smartly dressed, very attractive young lady enters carrying a tray of drinks: coffee and an entire selection of tea bags, bottled water, and several varieties of soft drinks. Class operation. Okay, now where are the light refreshments? No sooner thought than another lovely server enters, bearing a tray of goodies. Immediately I wonder where Ed hides these beautiful *assistants* during the day. No wonder all the doors are closed along the corridor. No red-blooded American male could concentrate.

My tongue must be hanging out, because I notice that I am the recipient of a rather severe look from Kristen. Quickly, I move to the beverage tray, empty two packages of sugar into a cup, and pour Kristen's coffee. Her acceptance is accompanied by the always-present smile. I am beginning to wonder if is the smile directed at me exclusively, or is it a permanent feature of her face? I guess I'm going to have to find out.

I select a bag of English Breakfast tea but quickly ex- change it for the more-favored Earl Grey. I want to show Kristen I appreciate the fact that she remembered. Pouring the water, I add the tea bag to steep. I always add tea to water, never water to tea. The latter method disturbs the leaves, often making the tea bitter. Also, if you use loose tea, the little leaves escape into the cup when you add water, and they invariably stick to your teeth.

It is time to turn my attention to more serious matters — the goodie tray. Why is it that the world as we know it may be coming to an end and I'm hungry? Maybe in a previous life I was a street urchin in Dickens' London and had to eat whenever food was available, for fear that there might not be any food tomorrow. Or maybe I simply like to eat.

Good taste frequently prevails over good-tasting. The goodie tray bears witness to the aforementioned theorem. I'm confronted with dozens of little crustless sandwiches filled with watercress, cucumber, undefined fish spread, and a paté of mystery meat. No wonder Yankees are skinny, they don't eat real food.

Kristen moves next to me and whispers, "This isn't really something we're supposed to eat, is it?

I'm in love, no doubt about it. I turn to face Kristen, and she is smiling. So what else is new, except that the smile seems to have real warmth. I am getting mixed messages — the cold, all-business façade versus the real live person underneath. I lean over to whisper something pithy, when suddenly Henry, who must have sensed the presence of his kind of food, announces, "We don't have any secrets here. It's firm policy."

Is he serious or is this an example of Henry's attempt

to be amusing? Notice I didn't say funny? I'm not sure. Anyway, the moment passes, but I am encouraged. I look at Kristen, who is blushing, a refreshing change from smiling. Maybe the end of humankind can somehow be averted, or at least postponed until...I almost slap myself. Having such thoughts at a time like this. In these circumstances, is a dying man granted his last wish? I'd better use the wish wisely. Maybe like giving me some, iddy-biddy clue as to where in the hell I am going to start.

These miserable excuses for sandwiches are beginning to look good enough to eat. Perish the thought! I pour myself another cup of tea. Hey, I've got to maintain certain standards.

CHAPTER EIGHT

The problem is far from simple. Where does one begin to find three people who have decided to vanish or have been kidnapped? I think I'm the only one considering the former possibility. Too many questions and too few answers.

"Are you okay?" I look over to see Kristen at my side. I wonder if I furrow my brow when I think.

"I just had a really bizarre thought, and I'm trying to put it into context."

"Maybe I can help?" Is she purring, or is my libido out of control?

While I try to pull myself together, I search for my deepest baritone voice. "I want to reconcile what we know with a series of hypothetical questions directed toward a motive." Sounds professional.

Absentmindedly, I reach for the sandwich tray. Thank God, years of training, combined with a primal instinct to avoid crustless white bread, causes my hand to stop, just short of the limp cucumber offerings. Yuck.

During this all too brief interlude, Robert again joins us in the conference room. What has he been doing the past several hours? Probably buying and selling companies, totally unfazed by the gravity of the situation. One must carry on. Stiff upper lip, you know.

"So?" Robert queries the assembled group. What a dumb opening. Like reading a pile of paper is going to solve this mystery? I don't think so unless asking questions is a sign of progress. I have a ton more now than I did earlier. No answers, but a lot more questions.

I bite my tongue to avoid saying something which would probably offend at least one of my employers. "Has everyone read these files?" I again hold up the now somewhat dog-eared binder. At least I'll get a feeling of who is on which page. Okay, I admit it's a bad pun. Everyone, except yours truly, has previously read the background material.

"Does anyone know anything that might possibly — and I don't care how remote the possibility is — add to what we have discussed or is in the file?" My question seems logical, at least to me. I am greeted with silence. Nobody knows anything. Nobody sees anything. The scene reminds me of Sergeant Schultz from the sixties television series *Hogan's Heroes*. He always heard, saw, or knew NOTHING! I don't buy it, but I'm stuck with it…for a while.

Here goes again. "Is there a chance that the disappearance was not an act of kidnapping, but a plan devised by Onellon, Gordon, and Kettleman to take off with essentially the economic heart and soul of the company?"

If my last question was met with silence, this suggestion is met with *absolute* silence. Not a creature is stirring, not even the acting CEO.

Everyone slowly regains consciousness and starts looking questioningly at one another. Clearly the notion that

Henry, Ed, Robert, and the others have been ripped off never before entered their collective minds. Funny how *rip-offers* never think that they might be *rip-offees*.

"But why?" Ed sputters. "They had everything: economic support, the confidence of the investors, a majority stock position, pretty much a free hand in operations. What more could anyone want?"

I don't dare suggest peace and happiness forever. "Maybe they wanted total control, the whole ball of wax and they didn't like reporting to you like school children having their homework checked." I don't like the tone of my voice, but I clearly strike a sensitive chord. Talk about crestfallen. The faces of the assembled literally fall, except for Kristen, who, like me, doesn't know the personalities of the missing men.

"Illogical!" Henry proclaims, sounding a lot like Mr. Spock of *Star Trek* fame. "It simply doesn't make sense." And why doesn't it make sense? And greed is a very powerful motivator. I am not making any headway. No one is saying a thing. I've hit a nerve center.

"Let me answer my own question." Everyone hangs on my next word, which may or may not meet with a positive response from my employers. "It is very unlikely, although not altogether impossible, that the three simply left of their own volition." I pause to judge the reaction. "First, it would take a great deal of planning and although these guys are bright, it would be hard to carry on an operation of this magnitude without someone getting wind of it. Whether it's making arrangements for travel, asking someone to water your plants, increased activity in bank accounts so that you can have money available, whatever, there is always something, which is why I think that it's something else." A collective sigh fills the room. I'm on a roll. "The Ebola is the key. Why take it? Or is it really gone? Or was it ever there? For insurance? For safety? For terror? Against what or whom? Nothing really fits. Unfortunately, the one thing we do know is that their research is gone."

We are really no further along than when I started down this apparent dead end. I was hoping that I could extract some additional information by rattling a cage or two. Anything that might possibly assist in finding the proverbial needle in the haystack. Not only am I exhausted, I am also really hungry…again. How can I let my *hosts* know without offending them? "If no one has any additional input other than what is in the file, then I suggest that we reconvene tomorrow morning at the GSS offices. By then I hope to have revisited everything that has been discussed so far."

I look around for reactions. To no one in particular, I add, "How can I gain access to their residences?"

Once again, I am greeted by silence. At last, Henry clears his throat. "It appears that all three men lived together in a rented home rather close to the GSS offices." What's the big deal one way or the other? Not only would their living conditions make working long hours easier without worrying about bringing the office home, but it would certainly facilitate making and executing a disappearance plan. Maybe I was a little too quick to dismiss that scenario. Shit. This keeps getting harder.

Kristen senses my increased anxiety level and offers to meet me at the GSS office at eight the following morning. She has learned from the GSS receptionist that the office custodian has a key to the rented house. Apparently he does odd jobs for the trio on his days off. Although the thought of meeting Kristen in the morning is quite pleasant, a leisurely dinner seems even better. How to broach the subject?

"I don't think it will be necessary, uh, useful, if Robert, Ed, or I join you tomorrow." Henry rises from his chair. "Although, and I speak only for myself, I will be reachable by phone throughout the day."

Robert and Ed nod in agreement.

Am I being given the bum's rush or is it that once I've signed on board, the money people can breathe freely since they've done everything possible? Or have they?

Are they simply washing their collective hands, in a manner befitting Pontius Pilate? I am beginning to lose some of the awe in which I previously held Ed and Henry. I look over at Kristen. She isn't smiling. Neither am I.

CHAPTER NINE

What to do? Go back home, order a pizza, reread the files, and try to make some sense out of this mess, or… Sometimes being alone at home at night is therapeutic, but more often, it is depressing. I need to rethink my life when I have time.

I wonder if there is something akin to subliminal dialogue. I mean, can my thoughts be intercepted by another person? I'm becoming a believer.

"Let's get a decent dinner. North End okay?" Kristen whispers, avoiding Henry's gaze. Not only does she pick the best area in Boston for fabulous Italian food, but it is within walking distance, romantic and very European. This woman is scoring a lot of points, but why? Stop asking too many questions, relax, go with the flow, although it is best to be careful. There's no one waiting for you at home; no dog to feed, no love of my life, and your sons are happily away at college. But what about completing all the work necessary to save the world? Well, we'll talk business between sips of Chianti.

I pick up my folder and address the group, hoping that Kristen will get the message. "I've got a lot of catching up to do."

Turning toward Kristen, giving her the best wink I can muster, I say, "See you at eight am sharp." I give a curt nod to Henry, Ed, and Robert. As I turn to leave, Ed graciously offers to see me to the door. *"Grazie,"* I say, turning to Kristen. One quick glance at her tells me that she understands. This subliminal communication is starting to scare me.

Ed and I shake hands in the reception area. He looks terrible. "I probably should apologize for not giving you a little more background. I put you on the spot." He looks even more remorseful than before. "If I felt the reason we hired you was to save the world from destruction, I could sleep better. Truth be known, it's a lot closer to saving our collective asses. Waiting three weeks was not only unconscionable, but it really has made your job so much more difficult. Steve, we really didn't know about the possibility of an Ebola situation until yesterday. The delay was corporate spin control. Believe me, no one ever considered that the world was being put at risk. If our investment simply walked out the door, our credibility would evaporate. We needed to keep this under wraps until we got some handle on what was going on. The reason we didn't make much progress appears to be related to the unknown factor of the Ebola. I'm scared shitless, absolutely shitless."

I've never heard Ed use a profane word before, much less twice. I shrug understandingly, but there is nothing I can say, except "I'll keep you posted."

That seems to immediately snap Ed out of his funk. "Please call at least twice daily. We want to keep the rest of the investors up to speed. Can you send us a written status report everyday?"

"Ed?" I try to be gentle. "I've got two days to stop Armageddon. I may not have time to do all the paperwork you want."

"Yes, yes, you're right. Just keep me in the loop as much as you can, please." Whoever invented the word *hangdog* was probably looking at Ed.

I reach for the brass handle to let myself out. It shines, reminding me of the tune from *H.M.S. Pinafore* where the fellow shines the handle on the big front door until he becomes an admiral in the Queen's navy. I need to get away from the offices of Capital Investments, LLC forthwith. You know, lawyer talk for *pronto*. Suddenly, I stop and wonder, what about Kristen?

I haven't even had time to consider my last rhetorical question when I hear, "Stephen, please hold the elevator for me." This woman has an uncanny sense of timing. I wonder if Ed notices. Forget it. He is so wrapped up in himself that he probably wouldn't notice if the fire alarm went off. Or would he? I haven't pulled a firm alarm since the fifth grade, and I don't think this is the time or place to revisit bad habits. I quickly push the down button as Kristen approaches, hoping that the doors will open sometime during the next hour or so. She reaches my side just as the chrome doors yawn open.

Standing at the back of the rapidly descending box, I struggle not to stare at Kristen. I focus on the little lights that designate each floor. I am so tempted to do something, but what? I really don't know anything about her. Maybe she is a spy assigned to see how easily my attention can be diverted. If she only knew just how easily. It's been a long time. My quandary is temporarily put on hold as the elevator comes to rest at the thirty-eighth floor and several very bored-looking people invade our space. Two stops later, I find myself shoulder-to-shoulder with Kristen. Even after a day in a stuffy conference room, she smells great. *Beautiful* or *Charlie*? A proper detective should know the difference, right?

Maybe in my spare time, I will hang out at a perfume counter and improve my olfactory recognition.

Oh well, if I ever have spare time on my hands, it will mean I've saved the world from destruction. I'd better concentrate. It's hard to do so, however, in a crowded elevator with a charming acting CEO standing next to you.

Kristen brushes past my arm as she walks out of the elevator. "Even hard-working world-savers are entitled to a few hours to enjoy a fabulous meal and a glass of vino."

"And don't forget the pleasure of your company."

Kristen lowers her head. I catch a hint of scarlet rising in her cheek.

Dinner is definitely going to be the high point of the day, unless I get really lucky and can figure out where to begin the investigation, find our missing executives, get paid, and schedule another dinner within the time allotted to solve this mystery — a mere couple of days. Better make this dinner memorable. It may be my last. A little bell is ringing in the back of my mind. A warning?

En masse, we all exit the elevator and head toward the revolving doors. I find myself out on the street, where it is dark and cold. I involuntarily shiver.

Suddenly, Kristen hooks her arm around mine. Probably to keep from being blown away. We turn and head for Atlantic Avenue and the North End.

As we pass my parking space, I notice that the good old Volvo now sports an orange ticket. I guess Henry's secretary forgot to put the quarters in the meter. That's a bummer. Add it to the bill. However, with Kristen on my arm and the thought of veal marsala on my mind, I don't care.

CHAPTER TEN

In any other city, strolling about half a mile along a harbor with a lovely lady on your arm would be as good as it gets. However, trying to cover the modest distance between Ed and Henry's office and dining in the North End is, how shall I say it an adventure? We encounter countless construction sites, endless traffic with the requisite horn honking, jaywalking, a Boston art form and some rather colorful language. None of the foregoing is conducive to romantic ambiance. Since Boston, often referred to as the *Hub* for reasons not related to city planning, is one of the oldest cities in North America. Its roads are more akin to rambling cow paths, which they were, than planned grids or rays emanating from a city center. Finding your way in New York City or D.C. is a piece of cake compared to Bean Town. In Boston, not only do the streets randomly meander without regard to the compass, they change names from time to time. And sometimes the street on which you are traveling doesn't have a street sign.

The overall strategy is, *if you don't know where you are, you have no business being there.*

We walk in silence, largely because there is so much ambient noise that we can't really hear each other. Part of me says that I should call Ed Harris and simply say I quit. It's only for forty-eight hours. No big deal. Maybe I'll learn something. Maybe I'll get to know Kristen better. I roughly estimate that the distance we're walking is close to two miles. The origin of the expression *as the crow flies* is taking on a whole new meaning.

Navigating around Jersey barriers and other obstacles is no easy task, but we ultimately wend our way to Hanover Street, gateway to Boston's North End. Although gentrification has claimed a bit of the quaintness of this uniquely Italian section of the city, one is immediately overwhelmed by the satisfying scent of spices; basil, oregano, and thyme; the sweetness of desserts: cannoli, gelato, and tiramisu; and the richness of freshly brewed cappuccino. Operatic music and the lyrical quality of the Italian language off set car horns and rap. We pass two elderly women, dressed in black from head to toe, sitting on a stoop, shawls drawn tightly against their frail bodies.

Kristen and I carefully examine the menus posted in front of the scores of restaurants that populate the area. We pass a small park, then turn right down a side street, hoping to find something less touristy — more intimate. Success! Trattoria Frascati. We climb up three steps to a lighted porch. We push open the huge wooden door, which swings freely on its well-oiled hinges. It takes a few seconds for our eyes to adjust to the dark-paneled room. Fifteen or so tables, all covered with red-checkered tablecloths, are strategically placed, leaving just enough room for wait staff to pass back and forth. We are almost knocked over by the infusion of wonderful smells, especially the omni-present garlic. A candle adorns each table, casting magical shadows.

We have just entered a place where time stands still. It has been years since I have seen real candles on tables. Somebody in the building department long ago deemed this symbol of civilization a fire hazard. The fancier, more upscale places in the Back Bay now use electric sconces or track lighting to create atmosphere, but not so in the North End, notwithstanding what some pantywaist inspector from City Hall says.

Those whose palates are not fully acquainted with real *Italian food* may not be aware of the fact that there is no such thing as Italian food. There are no less than ten distinct regional cuisines in Italy, including dishes from Piedmont (Turin), Lombardia (Milan), Veneto (Venice), Liguria (Genoa), Emilia-Romagna (Bologna), Napoli (Naples), Lazio (Rome), and Toscana (Florence).

"I love Tuscan cooking. It's probably the simplest of all the Italian regional cooking." Kristen uses her hands to emphasize each word. "It features the same passion for food that the Florentine masters exhibited in their art."

As we are being seated, I begin to feel a pang of guilt. Why is it that when I begin to feel good, guilt tries to rain on my parade? Hey, as my mother used to say, *You still have to eat* — especially if you are eating with a charming, witty, and very pretty woman who loves Italian food.

As the waiter eases up the chair behind Kristen, she raises her eyes to mine and says, "Relax, Stephen. You've got to eat." She either knew my mother or is reading my mind again. Both are scary thoughts.

I adjust my charm generator to the highest setting. It isn't hard. This lady makes me relax and feel good. I am going to try not to screw it up.

The waiter returns to our table with a bottle of wine. Not a wine list, but a single bottle of wine, which he shows to me with a flourish that can be executed only by Italian waiters. "Brunello!"

Without waiting for a response, he continues in an accent heavy enough to let me know he is not a native Bostonian. "This wine is from a small vineyard not far from my home in Montalcino. It is truly excellent. It is good with everything."

How can I say no? I can't. I don't. He opens the bottle in a well-practiced stroke and pours a little into my glass. Like the professional I am, I swirl the liquid and take a deep whiff. So far, so good. A taste confirms our waiter's recommendation. I grin in approval. He glides toward Kristen and fills her glass and then returns to fill mine. This place is already four-star in my personal Michelin Guide.

I lift my glass in toast to Kristen. "To life, luck, and love…not necessarily in that order."

Kristen's green eyes sparkle in the candlelight. "May we find what we seek and have enough time to enjoy it."

We each take a sip. Our eyes never part. Saving the world could wait a couple of hours. Anyway…we have to eat.

"It will probably make us feel a little less guilty if we talk shop during dinner," Kristen says. She reads me like a book.

"But only after we order."

On cue, the waiter reappears. "Ready to order?"

"We haven't actually seen a menu." I shrug.

"No? It's okay, I'll tell you what is best." This guy is my choice for *waiter of the year*.

"For starters, I think *cacciucco*." Neither Kristen nor I move. Picking up on the fact that we don't have the foggiest idea what he is suggesting, he continues. "Everything is from the sea. Fish, shrimps…and how do you say it…crawfish and mussels. Thicker than soup. You get one order and two bowls."

Simultaneously we nod. My mouth is already

beginning to water.

Our waiter does not even take a breath. "*Bistecca alla fiorentina*, the steak of Florence, brushed with olive oil. *Riso negro*…it's a black rice and some vegetable and perhaps asparagus. One order of everything, two plates. Plenty to eat." He turns and leaves us. Perhaps asparagus? I'm curious if each meal is individually created to satisfy the tastes of the patron. That explains why there are no menus. Maybe the meals are created to satisfy the tastes of the waiter. Fine with me.

Kristen raises her glass. *"Salut."*

"Here's looking at you, kid." Sorry, Bogey, I just couldn't resist. We'll always have the North End. Not quite Paris but a lot better than pizza alone in the suburbs. Wake up, Stephen.

Each and every facet of our dinner is incomparable. The presentation of each dish — exquisite. Each selection our waiter has made — wonderful. His sense of timing — perfect. Wine is poured at exactly the right time — an instant before the glass is empty. We savor each course-neither rushed nor ignored. It's as if we are special guests in someone's home. Trying to describe the taste of the food without experiencing the aroma and seeing the preparation — impossible. Suffice it to say, two hours pass by at warp speed.

Kristen says all the right things at all the right times, laughs at my horrible jokes, and seems to be truly enjoying herself. I also am given, between bites, a reasonably comprehensive analysis of post-disappearance GSS. Without Onellon and Gordon, it is basically a write-off.

We retrace our route back to Zero Financial Plaza. In order to retrieve Kristen's car from the basement garage, we have to reenter the building, sign in at the guard desk, show a photo ID, take an elevator to the parking level, and then walk to her car. Think about it, you sign in and then drive out. Who is to know if you ever leave the building? Maybe the *Terrific Trio* are stuck in some parking garage because they forgot to sign in.

Kristen never told me what kind of car she drives. I envision an Audi or a BMW. Nothing too flashy, but solid German engineering.

At this time of night, the normally crowded garage has but one car, a fully restored 1973 silver VW Beetle ragtop. No replica — the real McCoy. Kristen gives me one of those looks like, *What did you expect, a BMW?*

Oops! An awkward moment. Kristen extends her hand and says, "Tonight was really great. Thank you." She gives my hand a quick squeeze. "Try to get some sleep. See you tomorrow at eight."

She turns, opens her pocketbook, finds her key more quickly than I have ever seen a woman do before, opens the door, and slides inside. Rolling down the window, she says, "Want a ride to your car?"

It had never occurred to me how I was going to get out of the garage without a car.

"Thanks." This time I smile.

Walking around the back of the car to get in the passenger's side, I notice a window decal. It is a white oval with three black letters: *ACK.* I open the door and sit on the surprisingly comfortable seat. "Spend much time in Nantucket?"

"Whenever possible. My parents have a house in Surf-side which they never use, so my brother and I try to organize our respective lives to get there at least a couple of weeks each summer and some spring and fall weekends. Hey, how do you know I go to Nantucket?"

"A good detective never misses a conspicuously placed Nantucket sticker on a car."

For those of you who don't understand my deduction, ACK is the airport call letters for Nantucket. Not to be outdone by all the European countries (UK, FR, CZ, etc.), Nantucket created its own bumper sticker, appreciated only by those who are in the know.

"I spent nearly twenty years summering in Nantucket," I watch her buckle her seatbelt. "I had a decent law practice there, so I could work in Boston Tuesday through Thurs- day and spend four days on island, playing and working. It was a good life. But all things change. That's the only constant... change."

"Maybe if we locate our fugitives, we can take in a Madaket sunset or two." There is no flirtatiousness in her voice. Her eyes are directly locked onto mine. Where has this woman been all my life? Well, at least where has she been the last three years?

"You've upped the stakes," I say. "Saving the world is nothing in comparison to a couple of days on Nantucket. I guess this means we'd better get going."

Kristen winks. She wheels her version of *Herbie* onto Oliver Street and drops me at my orange-ticketed Volvo .

"Thanks again, Stephen."

This time I wink. "Eight o'clock, then." I close the door, turn, and walk to my car. A chilling breeze hits me and I shudder. I hope it isn't an omen of something yet to come.

CHAPTER ELEVEN

The ride home is lonely. Going home alone after an excellent dinner is a bummer. In a matter of ten minutes, I'm already missing her. This doesn't make any sense — or does it? The questions upon which I need to focus my fading energy and attention are clear. In descending order: where is the Ebola, where is the scientific data, and where is the missing management team? Trying to figure out why would be nice. I seem to require order in everything I do, but I am being paid for results, not to answer questions. I make a mental note to get a retainer — an advance against my fee. I'm not working on a commission or a contingency — based on results. It's dollars for each hour or fraction thereof, like the old days.

Having thrown my last four quarters in the toll basket, I exit the Pike into the relative darkness of suburbia. Maybe I should get an E-Z pass. No way. I'm happily still chained to the past and like it that way. My precious grass would never forgive me. Sadly, I'm still chained to the past, which wasn't so bad until the end.

I spend about twenty minutes trying to put various factoids on a legal pad — old habits are hard to break. I call it a day.

Sleep does not come swiftly, but when it finally decides to reach me, it seems as if only a few seconds pass before the alarm screeches in my ear. I am one of only a few remaining souls who insists on being awakened by an alarm clock, no music, no TV — just a plain, obnoxious alarm. I wonder if I can blame that on my mother, along with everything else.

Shower, shave, cup of tea, a firm brushing of the teeth, together with the mandatory flossing, and I'm ready to face whatever the day has in store for me. The weather is clear and warm, which means in New England in November, stretching to reach fifty degrees. I figure I will be in and out all day and, thus, layering is in order.

Shirt, tie, and flannels are the staple of my fashion diet, to which I add a sleeveless sweater and a Harris tweed sport coat. If the weather turns really awful, as it often does, I have stored in the trunk of the Volvo foul weather gear: rubber jacket and pants, collectively called a slicker by the souls who fish our waters, L.L. Bean boots, a trench coat, which every private dick needs, and an old but very warm parka.

I set out toward the GSS offices, hoping to find somewhere I can buy some bagels for breakfast. Recently, everyone has discovered what I have known for a lifetime, bagels are better for you than donuts. Where once a family-owned bagel shop proudly stood, alone in the sea of fast food chains, the bagel, like its sugary, holed cousin, has given in to the siren of big franchises. The likelihood that I will find a bagel is very high, but is it fresh?

I am not disappointed. I find a bakery with a *FRESH BAGELS* banner in the window. Finding a parking space is a snap because I have the whole strip mall at my disposal since at 7:30 in the morning, only the bakery is open. Entering is a big mistake, however.

I remember waking up every Sunday morning before anyone else was stirring, jumping into a pair of sweats, bicycling to the local bakery, and buying a selection of wonderful treats. By the time I returned home, the children, still in their pajamas, were up and watching TV, just waiting to see what Dad had brought them. That seems like a million years ago.

If last night's aroma was garlic and olive oil, this morning's is fruit fillings and frosting. Hey, you can get a bagel any day, but an honest-to-goodness old-fashioned bakery, now that's special. True confession time: I like food, but I love really good food. To me, eating is more than getting protein or vitamins, it's an experience.

The biggest problem I now face is, what does Kristen like? She seems very conscientious about what she eats, but where am I going to find something low-fat or sugar-free in a real bakery? What's the big deal? Just ask the patiently waiting clerk. "Do you have anything that not only tastes great, but is healthy, or at least not bad?"

I wait for his reply, half-expecting a baking pan to be thrown at me. What a dumb question! How can anything that smells so good be good for you?

"We have six different varieties of low-fat or no-fat muffins, and although I can't say with medical certainty they are good for you, I can say they aren't bad for you, and they taste fabulous."

"Give me one of each," I say.

"Do you want the low-fat muffins in the same bag as the no-fat?"

I think long and hard. If I put them in separate bags it will reflect my awareness of healthy foods. "Separate bags will be fine."

"That will be $9.70, sir."

Searching for exact change, I realize between the Pike and the parking meter, I have used up my precious cache of quarters. I hand over a ten-dollar bill in exchange for the bags and change, I thank the clerk and head for the door. The muffins really smell good.

The balance of the trip to GSS takes only about twenty minutes. I enter what appears to be a high-tech/biotech complex housing about thirty different businesses, each of which has a complicated name, simplified by a couple of letters in a fancy logo.

GSS is located in the fourth of six buildings — single-storied and brick-faced, with small windows and a loading bay to the right of the main entrance. Simple and very efficient.

The entire complex seems well-maintained and nicely landscaped. Picnic tables dot the grassy areas. Other than the signage, there is nothing to distinguish GSS from its neighbors. I grab my bakery goodies and briefcase and head toward the door. I give the handle a quick pull. Oops! Maybe the building doesn't open until sometime after eight. I ring the bell next to the door.

About a minute or so later, the new love of my life answers the door. I tend to exaggerate. This woman could wear a business skirt and blazer and still win a bathing suit competition.

"I brought breakfast." I hold my bags aloft.

"I'll make you a cup of tea and we can eat in one of the conference rooms. My desk is way too messy." I follow as she turns and walks through the reception area, consisting of three chrome-and-gray-fabric chairs, one metal secretary's desk and chair with computer terminal, phones, and a fax/scanner/printer/copier machine. No frills. The walls are painted white. The only decorative touch is a couple of Ansel

Adams black-and-white photos in chrome frames. Someone has a sense of understated value.

We pass through a door into the "executive" portion of the office. Each office is exactly the same. The name of the occupant is inconspicuously mounted on the side of each door. The furniture is — let's say — utilitarian. Basic desk, chair, credenza on which a computer rests, and a bookcase. No one has to worry about filling space with odds and ends. There is no room for anything or anyone, other than the named occupant. If you want to talk with someone, you go to a conference room, of which, I later learn, there are six of varying sizes, or repose to the lunchroom. The latter is where Kristen and I are headed.

Turning yet another corner, we enter a fifteen-by-ten foot windowless room. For a company with more than forty employees, I guess everyone eats at their own desk or at picnic tables when the weather's nice, since there is only one small table, four chairs, a refrigerator, small sink, microwave, coffeemaker, bottled water dispenser, and a cabinet in which I assume supplies are stored.

With practiced efficiency, Kristen finds a clean cup, adds hot water from the dispenser, and then reaches into her jacket pocket and produces a bag of Twining's Earl Grey tea. She pours herself a cup of what appears to be freshly brewed coffee, turns, and retreats from the snack room. It just isn't big enough to be called a *lunch* room. The GSS office layout favors the maze look — one wrong turn and you go from office to laboratory. Shit! I hope I don't get lost. I definitely am going to need a guide map.

Kristen opens the door to a conference room. One table, eight chairs, speakerphone, and a Starbucks cup with pencils in it. I'm not kidding. I don't know where the investors' money has been spent, except that it wasn't spent on furnishings. I place the bakery bags down on the table, the briefcase on the floor, and then relieve Kristen of the cups she is holding. Like the gentleman my mother trained me to be, I pull back one of the chairs for Kristen. She gracefully seats herself and allows me to give the chair the little push it needs to reach the table.

I hold up the bags, one in each hand, and announce, "Low-fat or no-fat?" I pause to await some pithy reply from the acting CEO.

"Blueberry," she exclaims joyfully, "whichever is blueberry." Searching the bags, I find a muffin laden with large blueberries. Damn, I forgot napkins. No sooner had I thought it than Kristen produces from her blazer pocket- napkins, which she purloined from the snack room while I wasn't looking. Being less selective, I reach into the other bag (don't ask whether it was the no-fat or low-fat, since I forgot to mark them, and I certainly can't tell the difference) and pull out a banana nut delight. The smell from this baseball-sized piece of pastry fills the entire conference room.

"Trade bites." Kristen is grinning.

I offer her my muffin. Instead of taking a small piece off the muffin and then eating it, she takes a bite. I detect some meaning in the gesture, but I'm not entirely sure what it is. I hope she's not a barracuda with great legs. Kristen extends her hand and offers me...her blueberry muffin. Needless to say, I take a bite. Our eyes meet, and we are both smiling.

Not wanting to destroy the special mood, but aware of the enormous task in front of us, I inquire, "Where should we start?"

She doesn't hesitate. "We should probably get the guy from maintenance who care takes the house to let us in. It's a beginning."

Kristen has put some thought into this investigation since last night...ah, last night. Stop it, Stephen, you need to concentrate or there won't be any more tomorrow nights, that's a certainty.

"As good of a start as any that I've come up with," I say.

Kristen reaches for the phone and dials a three-digit extension. "Ken, this is Ms. Marks. Will you be able to take us over to the house in say," looking at me, "ten...no fifteen minutes? Great. Thanks." She returns the handset to the cradle.

I swallow a mouthful of muffin. "Do you know if anyone has been to the house since the disappearance?"

"As far as I know, Ken went there the Tuesday following Columbus Day, about three weeks ago, to look around. Basically, at Ed's request. He said something about fixing a window, which he had planned on doing anyway. The following Friday, Ed, and I think Robert, went to the house with Ken to see if they could find anything."

"Find anything? What were they looking for? Don't you think that's like trespassing — maybe breaking and entering? And why were they looking in the first place?" I raise my voice with each question.

"I don't know. Remember, I didn't come on board until Monday, a whole week after the kidnapping or whatever." Instead of the usual smile, a frown of concern wrinkles Kristen's forehead.

I take a deep breath. "Did they find anything?"

Kristen shakes her head. "Nothing, I guess. I asked and they told me they didn't find anything. I probably shouldn't have, but I asked Ken later and he said they just walked around, talking to each other. He didn't pay much attention, because he decided to water the plants and make sure the heat was okay, and that the outside water had been turned off in case of a freeze."

"Has Ken been back to check on the plants since then?"

"Apparently not. He did tell me that he's driven by a couple of times because he feels somehow responsible, but he is nervous about going in. He told me yesterday that he feels he should check on the house, and I told him I would go with him, and...so we're going."

Looking deep into her emerald eyes doesn't make the next question easier. "Don't you think it's strange that the two lead investors of GSS enter the house of three missing co-directors to look for something which apparently they don't find? And more disturbing, that they never mentioned it to me at an all-day briefing?" I pause. "What were they looking for? It has to be something obvious. I can't see those two acting like Sherlock Holmes, without a very good reason. Something doesn't figure." I can't believe I was referring to Ed with such indifference and suspicion, since he was the reason I'm here.

"Maybe it was simply an extension of checking out the office to see if the computers had been moved to the house, or if there was something that might shed some light on what was going on. Remember, they didn't even suspect the Ebola might be missing at that point."

"Like a note saying *Gone to Hawaii for a couple of weeks, we'll send a post card.*" I sigh. "I'm sorry. It's just frustrating that there doesn't seem to be any thread to follow."

Kristen puts her hand on my arm, lighting up not only the room but also my spirits. "Let's go. Ken is probably champing at the bit to water the plants."

"Lead on...my dear."

I follow Kristen like a teenager following the prettiest girl in school. Not cool. At least my tongue isn't hanging out...I hope.

After rounding at least half a dozen corners, we approach a door announcing **MAINTENANCE**. Rather than boldly entering, as would be the right of an acting CEO, she demurely knocks. A tall man with short white hair, wearing a white shirt, blue tie, and chinos immediately opens the door. He could have been anything from an executive to — well, a maintenance man. The only real giveaway is the red rag sticking out of his back pocket.

Kristen extends her hand to him, saying, "Ken, I would like you to meet Stephen Blackman. He'll be going with us."

"I'll be r-r-r-right with you," Ken stutters. He turns around to scan his domain. Satisfied that everything will make it through his absence, he takes a ring of keys off a hook, snaps off the light, and turns toward us once again. "O-o-o-okay."

"Stephen, where are you parked?" The question seems a little silly, since there is only one parking lot. I'm so dumb. Kristen is very subtly telling me she wants me to drive rather than stuff us all into the VW or risk driving in whatever Ken drives.

"My carriage is out in front."

Ken shows a tobacco-stained grin at my weak sense of humor.

The ride takes about ten minutes, although it is only four miles. Traffic in and about the complex has increased as nine o'clock approaches.

We cross town lines and enter Concord. You know, like Thoreau, Walden Pond, Minutemen. Ken leans forward from the back seat, in which he insisted he sit, although he is the only one who knows how to get to the house. He points to a small road on the left.

"Turn there."

I execute the turn with finesse, which is the only way to execute a turn while traveling a bit too fast if one doesn't want to scatter gravel and otherwise upset passengers.

Ken points from the back seat. "It's the r-r-r-red brick

house on the right."

"Got it." I see a large, stately colonial home. Out of instinct, I stop, get out of the car, and walk to the mailbox. Not knowing what to expect, I pull open the mailbox door. Empty. I'm not sure what to make of that. Was the mail stopped at the post office? I make a mental note to check later. "Ken, did you ever take any mail when you came to the house?"

"No, sir. Never th-th-thought about it." Ken sounds sincere.

"Strange," I mutter.

Kristen turns to me. "What does it mean?"

"Not sure. Maybe nothing, but I doubt it." I guide the Volvo up the winding driveway. Nothing appears out of the ordinary. Maybe my theory that they simply took off isn't that crazy, especially if the mail is being held or forwarded. What about newspapers? There aren't any accumulated on the lawn or near the front door where I stop. Check the paper delivery service. Bet they get the Sunday *Times*. They probably fight over the Sunday crossword puzzle.

The house is quite different from what I had imagined would have been the collective taste of our AWOL executives. I had visions of a large contemporary, California-style, or possibly a smallish Cape. What am I saying? I have no idea what their collective taste in housing was…is. A center-entrance brick Colonial with a two-car garage. Sounds like standard issue for Concord.

We get out of the car and approach the front door. "The same key f-f-fi ts all the locks," Ken informs us. He unlocks first the top lock, which is probably a dead-bolt and then the second. We huddle around the door. Ken steps aside to permit Kristen to open the door and enter. As the door swings open, we all emit various descriptive exclamations.

"What in God's name…" Kristen sounds frightened.

" Holy shit!" I add.

"Jesus, Mary, and Joseph," Ken says without his customary stutter. The house is a mess. No, it's worse than a mess. It's a disaster. We carefully enter and look both right and left. The house hasn't been vandalized, it's been taken apart. As we walk through each room, careful not to touch anything, it's all the same. Every drawer removed from every dresser, bureau, and chest — bottom drawer first, so that each successive drawer can be stacked on top of the previous. The contents dumped and examined. Every pillow and cushion removed from its cover, sliced open, and then discarded. Every book and there are lots and lots of books has been removed from its shelf, leafed through, and thrown into a pile on the floor. There isn't a square inch of the house that hasn't been torn apart. The questions are threefold: what were they looking for, who were they, and shouldn't I call the cops?

"Kristen, we've got to call the Concord police," I whisper.

She shakes her head. "Do you think we call should Ed or Robert?"

"Ed and Robert were the last two people who we know were here. That makes them as much a part of the problem as the cure."

"I think we should l-l-leave, and I'll come back later to check on the p-p-plants, find this mess and call the police," Ken says.

Who is this masked man? I say to myself. "Ken, won't that put you at risk as a suspect or something?"

"It's all r-r-r-right. If you get bogged down with some of the locals, you'll never get to the b-b-b-bottom of this. I've lived around here for forty years. Everyone knows m-m-m-me. There won't be a problem."

"You are a surprise, a delightful surprise. Thank you." I am still troubled by the missing mail and newspapers, but

I keep that to myself. If Ken's idea is going to work, we had better get a move on it, and on the double. Kristen and I turn to leave.

Ken literally pushes us out. "I'm going to l-l-lock the doors again. Just in case."

In case of what?

"If whoever d-d-d-did this comes back before I do, it'll tip them off."

I wonder if everyone could read my mind. "Did you ever notice any computer equipment at the house?"

"They always carried their laptops in little black briefcases everywhere they went. No need for something else at home."

"Damn." I figure that the guys who tossed the house were looking for something computer-related — CDs or backup hard drives maybe. Everything is getting more and more difficult, rather than easier. Now I have third parties involved. I wonder if whoever made this mess abducted the missing someones but can't find the missing something. I'm beginning to think in riddles. I look around the room. These guys are pros.

We quickly retreat to my car. At least we're in a rural area, so unless someone is spying on us, the likelihood Ken's plan will work is pretty high. Shit, the thought that someone might be following us is creepy. I am in over my head.

"What's in the garage?" I ask Ken as I start to walk down the driveway.

"Their cars." He doesn't sound convincing.

"Can we get in?" I wish I knew when to stop and walk away. What's the expression — *curiosity killed the cat?* Great timing to think of that catchy phrase.

"Drive up real close to the door. I'll push in the c-c-c-combination."

As the door swings open, I am overwhelmed by yet another olfactory sensation, this one not so nice. The garage is immaculate and empty, except for two trash cans, one recycling box, and a fairly new Range Rover — the source of the smell.

Motioning to Kristen to stay in the car, I open my door and start to walk toward the smell. Ken quietly joins me. I almost gag. Ken pulls out his red rag and places it over his nose and mouth. Instinctively, I raise my arm to cover my face.

And then there were two. Sitting in the driver's seat is Theodore Gordon or what is left of him after sitting three weeks in a car, with a large portion of his head blown away. Close range, behind the ear — a little messy, but very effective. Pros.

I walk — actually run — back to the car, fighting off waves of nausea. I put one hand on top of the car, partially for support as I try to regain my composure. "Kristen... it's Gordon...dead...for a while. Please open the glove compartment and hand me my cell phone. Ken, I think I've got to call the police. Now!"

He agrees, or at least I think he mumbles agreement under the red rag.

She hands me the palm-sized phone and says, "The situation is out of our control, but regardless of what the police do, you've got to continue to try to get to the bottom of this."

"What is *this?*" It sounds like a reasonable question — under the circumstances.

"Stephen, we need to concentrate on why, and let the police look into who. The Ebola link, if any, the vaccine, no ransom note, and one murder. It doesn't go together. We need to look at places others won't. Ask the right questions. Please...at least for a couple of days. In addition to calling the Concord police, you're right, we've got to call both the FBI and the CDC, and then Ed and Robert. You've got to help coordinate everything and everybody. You can speak their language."

What she says makes sense, but what can I really do other than tell the authorities what I know — which may, or as I suspect, may not, be everything? I dial 911. The voice on the other end of the phone at the Concord Police Department isn't going to be thrilled to hear that this peaceful community is the scene of a murder.

"Concord Police, Officer Williams speaking. You are being recorded."

CHAPTER TWELVE

Within ten minutes, there are more flashing lights at the crime scene than the Fourth of July at Disney World. The first members of the law enforcement community to arrive are a pair of cruisers filled with Concord's finest, followed almost immediately by three state police vehicles. By pure happenstance, there is a state police barracks less than a mile away. The feds take a little longer, but only by minutes. By ten o'clock, a mere forty minutes after our initial arrival, there are a dozen official vehicles cramming the driveway, including the medical examiner, an ambulance, five marked squad cars, four unmarked cars, and, I kid you not, the Concord Fire Chief. Bad news sure travels fast in this sleepy suburb.

If it weren't for the seriousness of the situation, there'd be a carnival-like atmosphere to the place. I urge Kristen to stay in the car. She is really rattled. The color has drained from her face. All the business school training in the world doesn't teach you how to deal with a murder.

Ken surprises me. He seems to know everyone. As each wave of local or state cars arrives, the occupants invariably acknowledge Ken by name. I make a note to check up on this maintenance man.

It takes more than an hour for someone with authority over the diverse jurisdictions to emerge. A young, clean-cut man in a dark suit approaches me. I had expected the leader of this band of cops to be more seasoned. Maybe a little more gray hair.

"Mr. Blackman?" he asks in a polite tone. I nod. "Mr. Mays would like to speak with you."

That settles the question relative to the age. I am being escorted by a junior member of the team to the most senior. Why not? I follow my guide to a waiting silver Ford Crown Victoria — no markings — government license plate.

As I approach the car, the rear door swings open and a voice booms out, "Blackman...you're a tea drinker, right?" Before I respond, the voice once again bellows, "Fitzgerald... get Mr. Blackman a cup of tea. And try to get the good stuff. Blackman, please come in so we can stay warm."

I normally wouldn't enter a car with a stranger, let alone someone with the apparent disposition of its present occupant. Since there are no fewer than twenty law enforcement personnel within shouting range or is it shooting range, I think I'm either safe or in grave danger. Truth be known, I want to meet *The Voice*.

I'm taken aback as I enter the car. I hope I'm not staring. The Voice is an African-American man whom I guess to be about my age. He is very broad-shouldered and powerful-looking, but wears full leg braces. As I enter the car, The Voice extends his hand. "Deputy Director William Howard Mays, but you may never call me *Willie*," he says with a wide, warm grin.

"Deputy Director of what, may I ask?"

"Sorry. The FBI. J. Edgar's boys, Stephen. May I call you Stephen?"

What else can I do but nod in the presence of the deputy director of the FBI?

"I'll answer a few of your questions if you'll answer a few of mine."

I wasn't aware that I had asked any questions.

"I've been with the Bureau for almost thirty years," Mays continues. "I am the first disabled person of color to become an agent. The image of the FBI at that time was rather tarnished by the late and not-lamented former director, and it was widely thought that a young, bright, black polio victim would help recruiting. Three decades later, I'm number two, and I try harder."

I'm breathless, well, almost breathless. "What is the deputy director of the FBI doing twenty minutes from a previously undiscovered murder in Concord, Massachusetts, and why do you care?"

"Herein lies the problem. It is not entirely by accident that we're in the area. This conversation is going to take a lot of time, and this car is not altogether conducive to an interview. While I normally might suggest, rather strongly suggest, that we meet downtown, I am convinced that your role in this matter is such that the spirit of cooperation is going to be mutually beneficial. The bad news is that in order to confirm my gut reaction, I will need to interview Ms. Marks to make sure that your version is consistent with hers. That means that until I have interviewed each of you, I must insist that you don't speak with one another."

A knock on the window interrupts our discussion. Deputy Director Mays pushes the window button, lowering the glass.

Handing me a steaming mug, not a paper cup of tea, Fitzgerald announces, "Ms. Marks said you liked Earl Grey.

Sir, she is being very patient, but would like to know what's happening."

Mays aims his remarks at me as well as to Fitzgerald. "We need to set up a comfortable place where we can keep our guests away from each other temporarily, and speak with them individually."

He looks at me with a deeply furrowed brow.

"If your budget permits, why not rent a couple of meeting rooms at the Colonial Inn in Concord Center? It's nice, quiet, pretty good food, and nearby." I pause. "And it's handicapped accessible."

"See to it, Fitzgerald. I'll keep Mr. Blackman here so he can finish his tea. Make sure Ms. Marks is okay and tell her we'll get this straightened out in no time."

Get what straightened out?

"To answer your next question..." he says.

This is another question I didn't even ask.

"We've known that something was not quite right at GSS for several weeks, but we haven't known exactly what. We hope to find out from you what's going on."

I wonder if they're going to ask me what I know, or torture me until I tell them. In either event, the result will be the same. I really don't know a thing. "Dare I ask why the FBI knows or even cares about GSS?"

"To say we know all sounds like Big Brother is watching. However, when you consider the nature of the research being undertaken at GSS and the participation of a member of a foreign intelligence agency, it's worth keeping our eyes open just a little bit wider than normal."

"Shit, you don't know the half of it."

"But I shall in time." Deputy Director Mays beams with that remark. It's a little frightening. I take a sip of tea. Suddenly, my cell phone rings.

"Blackman Investigations." Some habits are hard to

break. "Stephen Blackman here."

"Steve. Ed." Ed Harris is screeching. "What's going on? I just got your message. What the hell is happening?"

"Ed, please be quiet. Theodore Gordon is dead. My quick assessment is that he was shot at close range in the side of the head. Probably a couple of weeks ago." Before Ed can reply, Mays reaches out his hand with his palm up. Imagine a person asking for something without snapping his fingers. I hand him the phone.

"Mr. Harris, William Howard Mays, deputy director FBI, here. I wonder if you might avail me of about an hour of your time later this afternoon, say four o'clock? I hope coming to the Colonial Inn in Concord isn't too much of an imposition. We can meet tomorrow at our offices in the Federal Building, but I think the relative anonymity of the Inn might be preferred. Fine…four it is. Of course, here's Mr. Blackman."

He hands me back the cell phone as if nothing has happened.

"Ed, I've got to go now."

"Steve," Ed pleads, "do you think I should bring a lawyer?"

"Definitely!"

"Will you be there at four?" Ed is virtually begging. Seldom have I heard a more desperate man.

I put the hand over the phone and turn to Mays. "Can I be there when you meet with Ed Harris?"

"Let me think about it."

Careful man, the deputy director is. Not a good time for my Yoda impersonation.

I speak into the phone. "I'll try. See you there, in any event." Unless I am in jail as some kind of suspect or something. Shit, this has become a real mess. I push the *END* button entirely too hard.

"If you promise not to make or receive any calls without my consent until you, Ms. Marks, and Mr. Harris are interviewed, I'll let you keep the phone," Mays says.

His voice is so matter-of-fact. No threat, just a simple statement.

I pause for a second to consider whether Mr. Mays has the authority to prevent my phone use. Probably not, but he'd figure out a way to arrest me as a material witness or whatever, and that would take care of the phone, maybe forever. I am reminded that options are not always what they seem. For example, asking a prisoner if he'd prefer death by a firing squad or by hanging. Great choice. With as much of a smile as I can muster, I raise three fingers in the air and say, "Scout's honor."

"Good enough for me." This guy is an anomaly.

"What about the maintenance man? Don't you want to interview him?" Misery loves company.

"It's not a problem. Agent Wells has already been debriefed," the deputy director says.

"So it's Agent Wells. Makes sense. Wait a second, don't tell me he didn't know about the house being trashed or the stiff in the garage?"

"He was instructed not to enter the house without someone from GSS accompanying him, except to perform a task which had been directly requested by the deceased, Onellon or Kettleman." I guess Gordon lost his name along with his life.

Who would know, after the trio disappeared, whether Agent Wells had been asked by them or not? This doesn't compute.

"By the way, he never noticed the absence or presence of either mail or newspapers. Good sleuthing, Stephen."

"But he had a key?" People who have caretakers for their homes expect them to enter from time to time, check on the heat. That sort of thing.

"We didn't want the fruits of our labor thrown out the proverbial window by some high-priced, fancy defense lawyer — breaking and entering or unlawful search is what he would call it."

Deputy Director Mays did things by the book. I should feel relieved, but I don't.

We are interrupted by Fitzgerald's knock on the car door. As the window opens, he says, "Everything has been taken care of. Local and state are taking care of the body, car, and garage. We've got the house. Medical examiner is a professor of pathology at Harvard. He's as good as they get. He'll have an initial autopsy report within twenty-four hours. We've agreed to share information relating to the murder among the three jurisdictions, and I agreed, reluctantly of course, to be responsible for coordinating the exchange of information." There is a creepy look of self-satisfaction in his eye.

"Good!"

Fitzgerald lowers his head about one inch in response to the compliment and retreats. "Mr. Blackman, if you would meet me in about ten minutes at the Colonial Inn, I would appreciate it. Ms. Marks will be with Agent Wells, who, by the way, thinks the two of you are very nice."

"Nice? Is that an official term?"

"Pretending to be a janitor with a severe speech impediment often exposes an agent to ridicule. He feels that since both of you treated him with respect, you are probably exactly what you appear to be. I trust his judgment."

"What do we appear to be?" I am really curious. I have spent the last four years trying to figure out who I am, and now, within minutes, this agent has me pegged for what I appear to be. Whatever that means. Why did I spend all that money on therapy?

"We'll talk, later."

He pats my arm.

Shaking my head in bewilderment, I leave the car and head back to the Volvo. I'm so far disconnected from reality that I don't realize I'm still holding my mug, and worse, that I have drunk the contents.

I see Agent Fitzgerald, catch his eye, and hand him the now-empty cup. "Thanks."

He almost smiles, takes the mug, and returns to whatever he had been doing. What was he doing anyway? It isn't even noon and I'm totally wiped out. I'm also hungry. I drag myself to my car. Where's Kristen? Shit, she's probably a wreck. Having no other viable alternatives, I open the door and slide in behind the wheel. On the dash is a white piece of paper. It's Kristen's business card. I flip it over. She has written a phone number, next to which is the word home, followed by one of those silly smiling faces.

CHAPTER THIRTEEN

Concord Center personifies a New England town, it's from a movie set. Two intersecting streets dotted with high-end shops, galleries, real estate brokers, and restaurants. At the corner of Walden at Main, a left takes you past a very exclusive private school housed in several white buildings with green shutters, dating from the Revolutionary War, while a right leads to a couple of grassy islands dominated by a marble obelisk dedicated to Concord's fallen Civil War veterans. The far end of Main Street is anchored by the Colonial Inn. A veranda wraps around the front and side of the gray three-story, wooden, two-hundred-fifty-year-old structure. It sprawls along almost an entire block, showing centuries of renovations. Old Glory proudly flies from its flagpole.

I ease the Volvo into the parking lot at the rear of the building, pull into a space next to Mays's car, which is appropriately parked in a handicapped space and turn off the engine. The persistent sound, which I had attributed to the car fan, doesn't stop. I close my eyes. The sound continues and is now joined by a pounding in my head. No doubt a delayed reaction to a four-Advil day. Maybe I'm simply hungry. I wish it was that easy. I am worried and tired and hungry.

I wait in the car for a few minutes, wondering whether Kristen has already been led into the deputy director's lair. Two minutes later, I get my answer as another unmarked federal Crown Victoria enters the parking lot. Fitzgerald alights from the passenger side and opens the back door, from which Agent Wells emerges, followed by Kristen. She looks terrific, despite our morning's ordeal. I can't figure out how she pulled herself together. I casually open my door to make it seem that our meeting in the parking lot is coincidental. I don't think I'm putting on a convincing performance. Agent Fitzgerald, who again appears out of nowhere, gives me one of those *if looks could kill* stares.

"You okay?" Not much else to say.

Kristen smiles her magic smile. I swear the entire area brightens. "Fine. See you later...I hope."

Although her voice is very clear, there was just enough hint of scared little girl that the urge to *rush over and hold her* almost gets the best of me.

Agents Fitzgerald and Wells whisk Kristen into the back entrance of the Colonial Inn. It probably took Mays' staff less than ten minutes to check out the building, secure the entrances, set up an interrogation headquarters, and hopefully, order some food. Why isn't the IRS as efficient as the FBI?

As my stomach growls for what seems like the thousandth time n the last half-hour, I wonder what kind of fare they've been able to plan for their captives on such short notice.

My question is answered within seconds after I enter

the main lobby of the Inn. Anyone familiar with what we Americans call antique buildings, in contrast to Europeans, whose buildings are measured in millennia, not centuries, understands that no floor is level, no wall is flat, and no door opens easily. The lobby of the Colonial Inn perfectly illustrates these architectural features. The wide-board pine floor visibly tilts, the walls wave a friendly hello to visitors, and even the front door momentarily sticks shut before a little hip check forces it to swing open. These comments are not criticisms, but truths, which lend themselves to the charm of New England. I suppose that if I wanted flat floors, straight walls, and easy-to-open doors, I could move to California. But the beautiful seventy-degree days there couldn't match the warmth of a blazing fire welcoming me in from the raw November chill.

The ambiance is somewhat dampened by the presence of several FBI types inconspicuously sitting in wing chairs conveniently turned to watch the entrance with — I kid you not — newspapers held up in front of their faces to block their ever-moving eyes, narrowed to slits. I am immediately greeted by a young woman whose attire differs from her colleagues' only in that she wears a skirt, instead of trousers, to match her jacket. She even wears a tie. No wonder everyone makes fun of FBI agents. They are so stereotypical. It'd be funny, except, of course, this is serious business.

"If you are hungry, Mr. Blackman, the deputy director has reserved a small dining room." Very icy cold efficiency punctuates each word.

"Sure…thanks." I can't figure this group out. It's as if they'd planned everything weeks in advance. Maybe they really did, and Mr. Mays was simply waiting for someone to fall into his carefully spun web. The spider can be so cunning and ruthless. Oh well, enough thinking, time to eat.

I am abruptly awakened from my daydream by the

female agent. "Please follow me, Mr. Blackman." Needless to say, I do as I am told. Baaaah.

CHAPTER FOURTEEN

Believe it or not, I hardly notice what I'm eating. It's not that it isn't good; it simply lacks something…or someone. I'm worried as hell.

Without a thought, I plunge my spoon into the dish in front of me. There's nothing there. I suddenly realize that I have devoured an entire Indian pudding with vanilla ice cream, usually a real favorite of mine, and I didn't taste a thing. What a waste. As I push back my chair to rise, Ms. FBI enters the room and asks if I want a cup of tea. Two things immediately strike me: Have I been spied upon throughout my meal? Likely. And am I am being singled out as a tea drinker? They've probably got a dossier on me. It'd make interesting reading.

"No thanks." I sound artificially cheerful. I wonder if I'm still employed. Maybe I owe it to Ed and Henry…and Kristen, to continue snooping. I figure the deputy director would have something to say about my course of conduct, although I'm beginning to wonder if I will ever be granted an audience with him. I look at my watch. Good thing I'm being paid by the hour.

Having thought rather than spoken those words, I am somewhat taken aback when Agent Fitzgerald announces that the deputy director can now see me. The sooner this audience is over, the sooner I can see Kristen, assuming everything goes well, which is an awfully big assumption, isn't it? The omnipresent Agent Fitzgerald clears his throat in a manner clearly reflecting his restlessness at my dawdling. As far as I'm concerned, I was contemplating, not dawdling. Probably a matter of semantics to the otherwise impatient William Howard Mays.

We climb the well-worn front stairs. With a little help from Hollywood, it's easy to imagine a bunch of the locals getting together over a draft beer in April 1775, wondering if the British were really going to leave the relatively cushy environs of Boston and pay a visit to Lexington and Concord.

The interrogation room turns out to be the sitting room of what appears to be the Inn's *presidential* suite. Good thing it's past the foliage season and before the Christmas season. These accommodations are probably booked years in advance. The room is decorated with period antiques — a Chippendale lowboy, an inlaid tilt-top table, a couple of wing chairs that look like they've never been recovered. Pretty impressive stuff. All the room needs is a roaring fire.

"Please sit down, Stephen." Mays is already seated behind an antique table in a straight-back wooden chair. I slide into one of the wing chairs. Guaranteed 100 percent original. Even my derriere can really feel the horsehair stuffing in the seat cushion.

"I've had a chance to speak at some length with Ms Marks. She is delightful and very professional."

Of the latter I have no doubt, and about the former

I need no convincing, however, it seems a little odd that a senior member of the FBI would refer to someone he has just interrogated as *delightful.*

"Ms. Marks provided me with a rather detailed account of what she knows. Since her association with GSS predates yours by a few weeks, I was most curious whether there was any background information she might have, or observations she might have made, which would augment your presentation. Alas, she offered little additional insight. For your information, she was not involved in any way in the retention of your services. That was initiated by Mr. Harris, with whom I will be speaking later."

I incline my head ever so slightly.

"Apparently Ms. Marks was hired specifically to provide executive expertise, in an effort to ascertain if GSS could remain viable without its founders. She was not charged with the task of finding the missing men or trying to find a motive for their disappearance. I'm convinced that Ms. Marks knows nothing more than she has disclosed. I'm also convinced that your knowledge of the activities at GSS do not predate the briefing you attended yesterday."

I am relieved that the interrogation is going to be limited to the last twenty-four hours or so. My short-term memory is still good enough that I should survive my Q-and-A session with the deputy director.

"Stephen?" Mays's voice softens. "How long have you known Ed Harris?"

Shit! He's going after Ed. I try to sound nonchalant. "Over twenty years." This is not going where I thought it would go.

"Prior to your engagement by GSS, when was the last time you and he spoke?"

"Ed actually called me two days ago to schedule yesterday's meeting." I pause. "Before that, we hadn't spoken for about five years, although he did drop me a note about four years ago, saying how sorry he was for me and how he felt bad. That was about it."

"It's been a rough time for you, hasn't it?" The deputy director's voice is either expressing real concern for me or he could be nominated for an Academy Award. I'm not sure which. Maybe both. Beware of FBI personnel expressing human emotion.

"It really was and I appreciated the occasional supportive note I got from people like Ed Harris. He has always been a stand-up sort of guy."

"And that's important...loyalty." Mays interlocks his fingers. His hands are huge. "Ah, back to the subject at hand. Ms. Marks reported that a dossier was given to all of the attendees at yesterday's meeting." I nod. "May I have a copy?" No beating around the bush.

"You know, your request poses a slight problem for me. I can assure you that you've probably got ten times more information on the deceased and the remaining pair than what is included in the material I've been given. But if you don't mind, I would rather you ask Ed Harris, when you interview him. If he says yes, it's yours. If he says no, all I can tell you is that if he asks me, I'll tell him to say yes. I will probably ask you to make a formal written request...you know, *in the course of an investigation*, or something like that."

"I understand perfectly," Mays responds, "and in light of what I am about to say, I'll support your decision whichever way it goes. For whatever reason, and I probably know several good ones, you seem to have the confidence of all the important people related to GSS. I want you — the Bureau wants you, to continue with your investigation as you were originally hired to do."

I know what Daniel must have felt like when they threw him in the lions' den.

"Mr. Mays, when I first heard about the assignment, I readily acknowledged I was in over my head. Not only were there no leads, but the trail is three weeks stone cold. Then, when I found out about the Ebola." My voice is rising in volume and pitch.

"Ebola?" the deputy director shouts. "What the hell are you talking about?"

For an instant, it looks like William Howard Mays is going to lose it. He starts to tremble, pauses and reaches for a glass of water.

"You don't know? Isn't that why you're here?" I feel my blood pressure rising. "That's the only thing that really matters, well, except for Gordon's death. I mean, the missing research is just lost profit."

In a terrific job of pulling himself together, Deputy Director Mays says, "Stephen, there is obviously a hole, a rather large hole, in our intelligence. Please tell me…now…as much as you can about the Ebola. And then, maybe later today or certainly by tomorrow, you can give me a detailed, as close to verbatim as possible, review of yesterday's meeting."

"In a nutshell, apparently Onellon and Gordon had expanded their research from anti-cancer vaccines into other areas. As I understand the nature of their experiments, they would reverse-engineer a disease. By isolating the cause, they hoped to find the cure. Well, actually the prevention. If the genetic signature of Ebola discloses a missing protein, then by adding the protein, the disease is neutralized."

"Yes, I understand the theory, but what about Ebola specifically?" He's getting anxious.

"Apparently, they were actually experimenting with Ebola," I say.

"So what? The GSS laboratories are state-of-the-art. They have every known safety device, cleansing filters, isolation rooms — the works. There are countless laboratories throughout the country that handle deadly diseases. It's neither uncommon nor usually of much concern. Get to the point!"

"The Ebola is kind of…like maybe…missing!"

"What are you talking about? Ebola doesn't go missing!" Mr. Mays shouts once again.

I can appreciate that, since I recall feeling the same way yesterday.

"Two days ago, they — GSS — found out that along with the disappearance of computer equipment, lab notes, and of course Onellon, Gordon, and Kettleman, a container of Ebola which was being used in experiments is gone. Well, *may be* gone. You were right when you said that GSS has state-of-the-art security. According to the time clock attached to the specially locked safety room in which the Ebola was being stored, an authorized person entered the room early on the morning of the last day anyone had any contact with the trio."

"Christ!" Mays looks like he is on the verge of a stroke. "Who took it? No, let's start with who was authorized to enter the room and how is the room accessed?"

"According to the information I have, only Onellon and Gordon could open the door to the lab. Not even Kettleman had access. It seems that no one really wanted access because of the crazy stuff that was stored inside. In order to get in, you needed a six-digit combination plus a scan of your thumbprint."

I'm trying to sound professional, but thinking about this nightmare is giving me a splitting headache. The dilema I now face is: do I tell him about GSS's lack of permission to store Ebola or wait until it comes up later? Maybe it won't be a problem. Fat chance. Blackman's first rule — if it can be a problem, it invariably will be.

"Will you excuse me?" Willie Mays starts to tap furiously on the arm of the chair.

I nod and say, "Do you want me to go?" He shakes his head.

Agent Fitzgerald appears from the shadows. He reaches his boss, helps him to his feet, assisting the deputy director into a back room.

"It'll be a few minutes. I'm sure I will be fine. Go downstairs and get something to eat or drink." Mays' voice, calling to me from the back room, has a lot less confidence than before.

CHAPTER FIFTEEN

My first thought is to find Kristen. Then all the other thoughts flood my brain or what's left of it. I promised Mays I wouldn't talk to Kristen until he finished chatting with each of us, and I didn't think this interruption constituted an end to our interview. I'm also worried about the intensity of his reaction to the Ebola. If he truly didn't know about the possible disappearance of the *plague*, then what the hell is the FBI doing in Concord in the first place? I wonder if someone did get a ransom note after all. Can't be. He'd know about Ebola and someone would have interviewed Ed or Kristen before now. Why wait for a corpse, especially a very ripe corpse? Instead of things making more sense, everything is making less sense. It's time for a reality check. Who knows more than he or she is letting on?

Before I beat myself up with imponderable thoughts, I think about Kristen. What if I accidentally on purpose bump into her? That wouldn't really violate my agreement with Mays, would it? I could also use a cup of tea. Actually, I could use a double Wild Turkey 101 — neat. Right. I'd probably pass out. Maybe that wouldn't be a bad idea under the circumstances.

I retrace my steps and enter our private dining room. Whenever you want to be alone, there is always a crowd. I guess even FBI agents have to eat. I search the room (not too hard when it's only twelve feet by fifteen feet). No Kristen. Maybe she is being held hostage by the *no longer speech impaired* Agent Wells. I look at my watch. It's almost three in the afternoon. I feel like a truck ran over me — twice. I'm sure that I look the same way I feel. It suddenly occurs to me that Ed Harris is scheduled to be here in about an hour. I want to get this show on the road.

To accommodate our comings and goings, the Colonial Inn has set up a buffet table: sandwiches, small danish pastries and three giant urns labeled *regular, decaf, and hot water*. I instinctively search the little basket for a recognizable tea bag. I'm disappointed that they all display the logo of our host. I try to read the small print on the side of the bag, which is getting more and more difficult. Next thing I know, I'll have to go to the drugstore and get a pair of those little half-glasses for reading. After squinting and moving the bag back and forth to find a focal point, I determine that orange pekoe is my only choice. Thanks, but no thanks. A stainless bowl filled with ice and various beverages resides at the end of the buffet table. At least the selection of drinks is better than the selection of teas. Just as I pull an ice-cold cream soda from the bottom of the bowl, I hear Agent Fitzgerald bidding me to follow him. Should I put the bottle back in the bowl or take it with me? Take it! I'm entitled. How I hate that word.

I return to the interrogation room. Given Mays' reaction, I decide not to ask what the hell was going on. He probably wouldn't tell me anyway.

The deputy director has resumed his previous position and motions me to sit down.

"Sometimes I get these incredible headaches, and I literally have to stop what I'm doing and lie down for a few minutes," he explains. "Oh well. Back to business."

William Howard Mays is either taking me into his confidence or conning me. I opt for the former, with very great reluctance.

"I must confess that your disclosure that Ebola is missing..."

"Possibly missing!"

"I thought you said it wasn't in the lab," Mays says.

"No! I said that it is possible that Ebola was removed from GSS. Since all of the computers of the missing scientists are gone, the inventory of what was in the secured lab is gone. Nobody knows for sure, except, I guess, Onellon."

"Rather disconcerting, not knowing if a dreadful bio-hazardous substance is in the wrong hands, right hands, or no hands." Mays sounds incredibly calm. Amazing what a nap will do. "Maybe I get headaches when my preconceived notion of the order of things goes amok." Nobody can sound that sincere and be acting.

"I simply can't refrain from asking the question — what is the FBI doing here?"

"It was simply a matter of time before you were going to insist on an answer. You probably know what I'll say. Notwithstanding standard operating procedure demanding that I refuse to reply, I will say that there is more going on than meets the eye, and on a need-to-know basis, I personally will keep you up to speed. However, in exchange for keeping you in the loop, I need you to promise that you will let me know immediately if you discover anything."

"With all due respect, sir, what can I possibly discover that the FBI, with all its resources, can't find out?"

"Embarrassingly, for starters, I didn't even know about the Ebola. Bottom line, I want you to continue to investigate the disappearance of both men and research, and try to get to the bottom of the Ebola situation. We cannot classify this as a kidnapping."

That answers the ransom note question but not the *what is the FBI really doing here* question.

"The police will investigate the murder. It is more than likely that there is a connection with the disappearance. We will continue to do what we are doing, which I assure you will have nothing directly to do with what you are looking into. If something turns up on our end that might help you, the information will be made available. I will make arrangements for all law enforcement personnel to cooperate with you. Agent Fitzgerald will be your point man."

"I readily admit, I'm still confused. It sounds like you're saying that nobody official can look into the disappearance without there being evidence of kidnapping. But doesn't the death of Gordon change all that? Like the possibility of some kind of terrorist participation?"

The deputy director sighs. "These are all things we will be assessing. Maybe technically we could broaden our participation, but I'm not sure it would yield results."

While this sounds all well and good, I'm still far from satisfied that I know what's really going on. "Haven't we forgotten something? Like something really important?"

"You mean the Ebola? What good would it do to bring additional agencies into the investigation? Find Onellon and Kettleman, and the Ebola will be close at hand. If anyone makes any demands involving the Ebola, then we bring in experts in handling and containing the material. If the Ebola is already in the hands of those who might use it in ways we wish not to consider, the issue is both prevention and cure. Right now, I've got to assume it's in competent hands or no hands at all. Otherwise we will drive ourselves crazy with doomsday scenarios."

He's reading my mind, yet again.

"Stephen," the deputy director sounds a bit paternal, "you've been through a lot over the past few years. You're smart, observant, and articulate. You can probably get the confidence of anyone who might have unique knowledge. People will tell you things they won't tell us. Because of your little revelation, time is of the essence and you're the guy already on the ground. I have faith in your abilities, as did Ed Harris. You are in no way under any suspicion...and neither is Ms. Marks."

I breathe a sigh of relief.

"Ed Harris, to the best of our knowledge, is also free of suspicion, although he seems to be so involved that I can't really be a hundred percent sure. For that reason, and because he trusts your judgment, I am asking you to leave quickly and not to try to contact Mr. Harris until tomorrow. In fact, I suggest you not resume your investigation until the morning — after we meet. Coffee...I'm sorry, tea in my office at eight-thirty, old Federal Building, downtown. I'll have initial crime scene reports and maybe even the autopsy report."

I move my head hesitantly up and down. I guess my morning dance card has been filled.

"Oh, by the way, Agent Wells drove Ms. Marks to her car. She said you have her phone number and asked that you call her."

"Okay. Well, tomorrow at eight thirty it is." I turn to find Agent Fitzgerald entering. He holds the door, feigns a smile, and inclines his head about an inch. I guess that's the official way to say *bye-bye*. I am sure the room is bugged, although it would be totally illegal. Although Mays may be a stickler for legal technicalities, he didn't become the deputy director of the FBI without covering his butt.

I walk out to the parking lot, wondering if in my absence, a squad of agents searched every inch of the Volvo. I sincerely hope I don't have any unpaid parking tickets in the glove box. Damn! I just remembered the ticket that I got yesterday afternoon. It seems like a month ago. I rub the sides of my head. Headache from hell. Where is that card Kristen left me with her phone number?

CHAPTER SIXTEEN

I unlock my car and immediately, almost frantically, start to dial Kristen's home number. Suddenly I realize that a cell phone is far less secure than I think, especially a cell phone the FBI knows you have. I push the *END* button, sit back and take my first deep breath of the day. Less than forty-eight hours ago, I was blissfully ignorant of GSS, its founders, investors, and employees. But without them, I wouldn't have met Kristen.

Weighing my options carefully, I decide to start the Volvo. Step one. I ease it out of the parking lot. Now what? If I turn to the right, I will be heading north, through neighboring Carlisle and eventually to New Hampshire. Left will take me back to Concord Center. Guessing that Kristen lives closer to rather than farther from Boston, I head into the center of town to search for a pay phone. If I hadn't been such an idiot, I would have realized that when she wrote her number on her card, she didn't include an area code.

In the greater Boston area, Ma Bell or her baby, Bell Atlantic, now called Verizon for reasons unknown to me decided that two area codes weren't enough, four seemed like a better number. The telephone company wanted to add further chaos to our lives by randomly placing towns into an area code, so you really can't tell where someone lives by looking at the phone number. Now that there are four, almost everyone includes the prefix unless, of course, you've lived in Boston at least twenty years. In that case, most people know that if no area code is mentioned, it's 617, which in turn defines a rather narrow geographic area: Boston and a few surrounding towns. You've got to envy people who live in Rhode Island. They've got only one area code for the whole state.

Because I've lived in the Boston area since the sixties, when letters were used in phone numbers, I'm able to deduce — I love that word, especially now that I am a real live sleuth — that Kristen lives in Cambridge. This fact translates into two immediately important details: taking the left turn out of the parking lot was the correct move; and depending on when her interview concluded, and further assuming she didn't return to the office other than to get her car but headed directly home, she should be there by now. Lots of assumptions and you know what they say when you assume something.

I haven't even factored in traffic. What if she has other plans? Like a date? In the course of one minute, I go from euphoria to depression and drive right past a pay phone.

I decide that I should go home anyway: check the mail, messages, maybe take a hot shower and otherwise try to pull myself back together. Down Route 2 to 128. Down usually means south, unless you are traveling downeast (Maine) and then down is north. Isn't New England quaint?

Twenty minutes later, I enter the so-called *downtown*

shopping district of my cute little suburb. One hardware store, post office, a real barber shop, two banks, even an insurance agency, gourmet food store that is never open after seven o'clock, which is when I want to buy something for dinner, and a white-bread grocery store featuring high prices, average quality, and limited selection. We don't even have a gas station.

Waving at neighbors whose names I've long since forgotten, if I ever knew them in the first place, I turn in to the post office parking lot. It seemed to me that a post office box would be more impressive than using my residential address. Also more costly and a lot less convenient.

During the last couple of years, I have given a lot of consideration about whether I should stay in *vanilla land*, as I sometimes call home, or move into Cambridge. On occasion, I've considered having the world's biggest garage sale, taking only what I can wear, and heading out to Santa Fe, New Mexico. Why Santa Fe, especially since I haven't been there in thirty years? Beats me. I even went so far as to call a real estate broker, who sent me a color brochure of listings. Wow! Prices are almost as expensive as Boston. Apparently, Santa Fe is really in, especially with the high-end California types. Maybe Butte, Montana?

Time for a reality check. No mail! Go home, take a shower, pour a glass of wine, and call Kristen — in that order. Need to get psyched for the phone call to Kristen, and get cleansed from the day's events.

I pull in to my driveway, half expecting to find yet another official-looking car awaiting my arrival. Although Deputy Director Mays gave me the night off, I have received no such assurances from either the state or local cops who are investigating the murder of Ted Gordon, whose body I found, whose disappearance I've been investigating, and whose house has been tossed. I know how all this is supposed to work, but there is still a pervasive environment of interagency mistrust.

More competition than cooperation. I am relieved the coast is clear. A hot shower awaits.

As soon as I enter the kitchen, the phone rings. Shit. Why can't a guy get five minutes' peace? "Blackman Investigations."

"It's Kristen."

My heart starts to pound. "Hi!" I try to sound cool and casual. "I just walked in and was about to call you." Should I tell her about the shower and glass of wine? Nah.

"It certainly was one of those days I don't want to repeat too soon." She sounds like all the violins in the Boston Symphony Orchestra playing in sweet harmony. Too lyrical.

"Too soon? If I never have a day like today…ever, I'll be thankful."

"But in your line of work, you must have to deal with a lot of really unpleasant things."

How am I going to tell her this is my first real detective case? Probably I won't. Trying to be sincere without sounding dumb, I say, "No matter what, you never get used to the sight of a dead man." I think that came out okay.

For what seems like an eternity, neither of us says a word, then in perfect unison we blurt, "Would you like dinner again tonight?" We laugh.

Being an assertive male, I repeat my offer. "It has been a very long day, but it's finally over." I hope I don't jinx anything. "I'd love to have dinner with you. Do you like Indian food? There are a number of Indian restaurants in Waltham that are really great."

"Without seeming too pushy, how about a salad, and some Chardonnay in front of a fire…at my house?"

"You're on, if I can bring the wine," I answer. I feel like I'm back in high school and the prom queen has just asked me to dance. Two left feet.

"Eight o'clock, 21 Frances Avenue, off Kirkland."

"Know the area well."

"Park in the driveway, since I presume you don't have a sticker." Cambridge requires resident parking stickers in most areas, especially around Harvard Square.

"Kristen..." I pause. "You were great today." Suddenly I'm feeling flushed — embarrassed. She probably thinks I'm corny. Now there's an expression that really dates me.

"So were you, Stephen. See you at eight. I've got to get ready. Girl things, you know." She hangs up.

I pinch myself to see if this is all a dream. Why should it be? I did do a good job today, I'm reasonably bright and can be charming as required. Why shouldn't an attractive acting CEO ask me over for dinner? Let me count the ways. I don't want to go there. Suffice it to say, I'm pleased with the invitation and will do my best not to blow the evening.

CHAPTER SEVENTEEN

Decisions…decisions…decisions. At least I am down to two: shower first and then wine, or a glass of wine and then shower. Thank God Kristen called. Can you imagine if I'd been confronted with three tasks? In a decisive move, I opt for the shower first, then wine, then get dressed. Damn it, that's three.

Completing both tasks one and two, I stare into the mess I call my closet and make what I hope is an appropriate selection. I don't want to give the impression of being stuffy (coat and tie), but I'm not the turtleneck type either. Once again, compromise is mandated: blue shirt, sweater, chinos, and loafers. I'll just look like every other over-forty type in Harvard Square and probably mark myself as an old grad. I guess I'll never be able to run too far from my roots.

A moment of contemplative bliss is disturbed by the ringing of the phone. I began to experience what I fear is the beginning of a panic attack. What if it's the state police and they want to see me, like now? I look at my watch. I have to be in Cambridge in just over an hour. It will take about thirty minutes to drive to Cambridge, so there's no way I can go anywhere and be on time for Kristen. The phone rings again. Shit! Maybe I should let it go to voice mail. With my luck, the police have staked out my house and already know I'm home. They're waiting at the end of the driveway. Another ring.

I reach for the phone. "Hello." I completely forgot about the formality of Blackman Investigations.

"Is this Del's Pizza?" a ten-year-old voice squeaks.

"You've got the wrong number." I try to sound cheerful, and am so incredibly relieved that I almost start to laugh.

"I'm sorry, Mister. Bye." The kid sounds angelic.

I decide that if the phone rings again before I leave, I won't answer, even if it's the governor. Why would the governor call me in the first place? No sooner do I finish the thought than the phone rings again. Maybe it's Kristen, and she needs me to pick up something for dinner. Shit! Maybe she's canceling. I grab the receiver.

"Blackman Investigations."

"I musta dialed wrong again," the pizza-ordering young voice says.

I sound altogether too much like the dad I am. "Maybe you should ask your mommy or daddy to help you."

"They're not home. My brother and me are really hungry."

"Can your brother help?"

"No, Mister, he's only five."

"How old are you?" I'm getting involved.

"I'm nine," he or she responds. At that age, gender is not reflected in the voice.

"When are your parents coming home?"

"I don't know." Do I detect a sniffle?

It finally occurs to me that I can check caller ID and find out where these children live and call the police or something. *ID blocked*, it reads.

I need to keep the child on the phone to get at least some information.

"Hey, Mister, do you know the phone number for Del's?"

"You know, I've got a phone book right here, and I'll look it up for you." I quickly flip through the Yellow Pages under *PIZZA*. Hopefully I can find the town in which they live, assuming people order their pizza locally so that it arrives hot. I'm starting to panic. I can't find Del's in the suburban west listing.

"Where do you live, so that I can look up Del's?" I cautiously inquire.

"Mommy told me I can't tell strangers where I live," he or she remarks. Smart kid.

"Do you know where Del's is?"

"Everyone knows that Del's is in the Center, next to the movie theater." Based on the kid's response, he or she must think I'm really dumb. Not far off.

I don't know a single town around here with a local movie theater. Everything is in megaplexes in megamalls. More panic setting in. Two small kids alone and I can't figure out where they are, let alone how to get them help.

My mini phone friend suddenly shouts, "Gotta go, Mister, Mommy and Daddy are back." The phone goes dead.

I can't believe I just got myself all worked up over a situation in which I had no business getting involved in the first place. Am I doing the same thing with GSS?

Forget the phone. I open my refrigerator and start to check out my rather modest selection of white wines. Chardonnay, she requested. Can't go wrong with Kendall-Jackson Reserve. Since it's not cool to carry an uncovered bottle of wine, I open my infamous junk drawer into which I stuff everything I can't figure out what to do with. A little rummaging produces a nice bag with yarn handles, into which I slide the wine bottle. Although flowers would be a nice touch, finding a florist open after seven on a weekday is difficult even in Boston. In the *'burbs* — impossible.

CHAPTER EIGHTEEN

Selecting a route from my house to Cambridge is a challenge in itself. While the Mass. Pike always presents itself as an option, the only Cambridge exit is rather inconvenient to Harvard Square. Route 20, which sounds like a real highway but isn't, meanders through Waltham and Watertown, and at last count features thirty different stoplights, none synchronized with its predecessor or its successor.

I elect Route 2, a multilane road up to the Cambridge city line. At this point, it abruptly begins to weave along through a series of rotary intersections, which Bostonians attack with zeal. Since most Bostonians don't really know how to drive, rotaries are really exciting. Traditionally, the right-of-way is granted to the vehicle already in the rotary. In Boston, the most aggressive vehicle goes first. Signage has recently been placed at the entry of each rotary, telling drivers that they must yield to cars already in the rotary. This hasn't helped a bit.

Route 2 is so heavily traveled by daily commuters that tire grooves have formed in the road surface, creating a track, like cross-country skiing. Changing lanes means going from one rut to another rut, while you try to hold your steering wheel. Between potholes and ruts, Boston is the wheel alignment capital of the world.

Rather than challenge the rotaries, I opt to drive down Massachusetts Avenue a/k/a Mass. Ave., through North Cambridge. Once the bastion of former House Speaker "Tip" O'Neill and his cronies, the area is being gentrified by thirty-something investment banker types with young kids, who want the urban experience, the Harvard ambiance, the roomy Victorian houses and can pay the outrageous prices these unheatable monsters demand.

My favorite Mass. Ave. building is no more. It wasn't a boutique or a restaurant, but the best bookstore I've ever entered, and I have browsed more than my share. Kate's Mystery Bookshop was a detective novel reader's equivalent of heaven. At Kate's, you could find almost every great, good, or not-so-good mystery ever written. Better yet, if you were looking for something, anything, you could ask Kate.

Passing through Porter Square, immediately north of Harvard Square, sends waves of nostalgia over me. I spent over a decade in this neighborhood while in college, law school, and starting a job, so that I could earn enough money to move to the suburbs. Fond memories of an easier and a much more carefree time and place.

The area between Porter Square and Harvard Square has changed little over the last few decades, although the Sears building now houses several restaurants and Lesley University. While individual shops come and go, in the mile between the squares, one can find almost anything, from designer dresses to high-tech bicycles.

Two cars make left turns from the right lane without

the benefit of turn signals. It's evident that I'm back in Cambridge. There's no question that I'm out of practice.

I instinctively allow ten feet between myself and the car in front of me. Almost, but not quite, enough room to be cut off .

Although I don't have the exact statistics, I recall reading that more fender-benders take place in the greater Boston area per square mile than anywhere else in the country. I don't think it's the density of traffic. Surely there are more cars in New York City. It must be the caliber and disposition of the drivers. No big surprise.

I know where Kristen lives, within a couple of houses. Since I used to rent an apartment in the neighborhood, I don't experience typical tourist withdrawal. That sense of impending doom that arises when you can see your destination but can't get there from wherever you are. I'm in control. A left at the top of the square, a right into the underpass, a left at the fire station, a right onto Kirkland and a left onto Frances Avenue and voilà, I arrive. Why do I suddenly feel nervous? It's been awhile. Too long. Like a beautiful, intelligent woman invites me to her house. What is there to fear? Let me count the ways.

Hey Stephen, you only met this lady a day ago. Granted, it's been one unbelievable day. Be cool. Remember, she's acting CEO of your employer. Just go with the flow.

I must see someone about these conversations I keep having with myself. I guess I've been alone way too long.

I slowly inch my way up Frances, scanning each front door to find number 21. Needless to say, the houses are not well-marked, and it's dark. Like a beacon shining through the fog, Kristen's VW sits in the driveway of what must be her house. I pull up behind her car, take a deep breath, reach for the bag with the wine, and slink toward the door. I suddenly remember that I'm in Cambridge. Better lock the car. That is, if I want to find it again.

Kristen is watching my little dance, because as I head back to lock the car, her door opens and she steps onto the porch. "Stephen?"

"Hi." I try to sound nonplussed. "I forgot to lock up."

"Come in before you get cold." Her voice could melt ice. "I think I've got a pretty good fire going."

All I can think about is Fred Astaire singing the Irving Berlin tune or is it Cole Porter, *"Heaven, I'm in heaven..."* I tender my wine to Kristen and give her a little too-long kiss on the cheek. Patience...and caution.

CHAPTER NINETEEN

Elegant, but warm, gracious and understated. Not only does this describe the interior of Kristen's home, but it seems like a good way to describe Kristen herself.

People often think of Victorian houses as huge gingerbread boxes with fourteen-foot ceilings and lots of wood paneling. I think that *Upstairs, Downstairs*, the British dramatic series which put *Masterpiece Theatre* into almost every living room in the country during the late '70s, is responsible for most Americans' perceptions of the nineteenth-century architecture. The fact that Queen Victoria ruled England from 1832 until after the turn of the twentieth century allowed for the development of countless stylistic characteristics in period houses both here and across the pond.

Kristen's home is perfect with just the right amount of everything. The rooms are well-proportioned and many have wooden wainscoting, some of which has been painted, while some remains a rich mahogany color. Bookcases line walls not already covered with the most eclectic collection of art I have ever seen in a residence. An African tribal mask hangs proudly next to a Hudson River landscape. A signed Dali print is wedged between a nineteenth-century portrait of a dour lady. I hope she isn't one of Kristen's long-lost relatives. As strange as it seems, everything works well together.

The books that fill the shelves look as if they have been read with loving care. Paperbacks sit beside leather-bound volumes. The lighting and the furniture in both the living room and den are conducive to relaxed reading. The fireplace glows with warm, beckoning flames. The ceilings are higher than in more modern houses and are completely covered with elaborately stamped metal sheets.

I must be staring up, because Kristen remarks, "Tin ceilings were originally installed to reflect the heat from the fireplaces into the room. The problem was that they were heavy and would often sag. Also in damp climates, the panels will rust, but here in Cambridge, tin ceilings are still very popular."

Smart *and* beautiful, along with the ability to know my thoughts. What else could I ask for? I am getting way... way ahead of myself.

"Stephen? Would you like a drink or some wine?"

I snap back into here and now from wherever I've been.

"Whatever you're going to have." I attempt to sound like the perfect gentleman.

"If you're not in too much of a hurry for dinner, let's have a glass of red wine and sit down in front of the fire." No question — the woman *can* read my mind.

I follow her toward the kitchen. The butler's pantry has been converted into a small wet bar. She pulls a bottle from the wine rack and hands it to me without reading the label.

"Glasses are in the cabinet on the left, and the wine opener is by the sink. I want to give the soup a look-see."

The glasses are neatly arranged by size and shape. So as not to appear lacking good manners, I remove a pair of the properly shaped goblets and look for the wine opener. What I find instead, conveniently mounted next to the sink, is a machine that looks like it originally came from the dungeon of some medieval castle. I place the bottle into a cradle-like contraption, grab the handle, push it into the cork, and then pull the handle. It works! Not a drop spilled. Wow, I want one for my birthday.

"I think you'll like the wine." Kristen is working at the stove. "It's from Argentina — dry, full-bodied, and quite inexpensive."

How does she know what wine she handed me? I hustle back to the wine rack and start looking at labels to see if she had simply stocked up on a case of all the same label. No. Each bottle is different, and I don't see any recognizable pattern of placement, like by region, country, and type. She just knows.

I'd better shut up and pour. No sooner have I done so than Kristen whisks in from the kitchen, gently takes a glass from my hand, clinks my own glass, and says, "Cheers!" She grabs my free hand in hers and leads me back into the living room. I don't resist, even a little. Why should I? Is that an internal alarm I hear?

Kristen selects a chair near the fire, rather than the couch that would accommodate both of us. Should I read anything into it? It's too early to be sensitive.

"Would you mind putting another log on the fire?" She crosses her legs in the chair. "I'm beginning to feel the effects of the day."

I find a likely candidate and place the formerly proud maple tree, or a portion thereof, onto the fire.

"You'll burn yourself!" Kristen yells.

"Don't worry, I do it all the time. For whatever reason, probably dumb luck, I have never burned myself tending a fire."

Mounted next to the fireplace is probably the most clever device ever invented for fire lovers: a brass blow tube. It is a hollow tube, about three feet long, flared at the top and pointed at the bottom. One simply aims the tube at the base of the fire and blows through the mouthpiece. Any sluggish fire is instantly brought back to life. It sure beats sticking your face into the logs and trying to rekindle the embers by hyperventilating.

With the fire properly restored, I assess the situation. What is the appropriate seating arrangement? I select a less-than-inviting wooden chair and move it close to the fireplace — opposite Kristen, who immediately smiles and says, "Unfortunately the couch is too far from the warmth of the fire."

I shrug.

"It seems rather strange that despite the fact we met less than two days ago, I'm very comfortable with you. Maybe it's the intensity of the experience we've shared. On one hand, it's a little scary, and on the other hand it seems natural."

I start to sweat.

"I don't know anything about you, other than your basic résumé. Ed's been rather closed-mouthed. You know even less about me." Although she speaks softly, her words strike a sensitive chord. Basically we don't know anything of substance about the other.

"There are three ways to look at this." I straighten myself in the wooden chair. "One is that the world is coming to an end and we really don't have the time to get to know each other's past. Second, if we are going to save ourselves and everyone else on planet Earth, we still don't have time for small talk, at least until we've completed *Mission: Impossible*.

As a third alternative, and probably the option I choose, a person's background is only a partial reflection of who the person before you today really is — good and bad. How each of us got here is less important than where we are going."

"Wow, that was a mouthful."

I turn at least four shades of red. I wonder if I've crossed the line.

"Maybe now is a good time for dinner, so I can remove my foot from my mouth and insert a spoon or something."

She rises from her chair, walks toward me, and plants a warm and moist kiss on my mouth. She immediately pulls away. It's a control thing and I'm not the one in control.

"You're sweet." By now, I am putty in this woman's hands. I'd better save the world.

Kristen gently leads me to the kitchen. "I'll serve and you open the Chardonnay."

I remember! Irving Berlin wrote *Cheek to Cheek*. Lobster bisque, Caesar salad, French bread, wine, and her company — there's simply no better way to spend an evening. In fact, almost three hours have flown by before I even think about time, of which we may have precious little. We never speak about the past. Nevertheless, I learn an amazing amount about Kristen. Her taste in music, art, literature, and theater, which when juxtaposed with mine, covers just about every facet of the art world. While our preferences seem different, we always share one or two characteristics. Her preference in art is much more modern than my rather pedestrian love for impressionists, although those few modern painters whom I like, she adores. Her tastes in the performing arts are more for dance and ballet, while mine are clearly rooted in Broadway shows. I can't get over the fact that we both like the same things in each other's area of preference. We seem to have similar taste in literature and music. Kristen and I both read avidly, and our shared musical tastes go from Vivaldi to Cat

Stevens to Pink Floyd.

We don't speak about former relationships, family, or friends. Whether we each make a conscious choice or not, I'm not sure. It just might be that we are more comfortable talking about mutual interests than talking about other people.

Simultaneously we get up from the table to clear the remaining dishes. One clear sign of how much talking we had been doing is the fact that there is some wine remaining in the bottle. Definitely unusual where I am concerned.

How do I avoid committing a potentially relationship-ending blunder? Like how to leave? Change the subject? Help in the kitchen? Yawn? True to form, Kristen supplies the answer.

"Stephen, I've been thinking about what you said earlier, and I am betting that the world won't end, and that there will be time for all sorts of things later on. I want you to know how much I enjoyed this evening. I can't remember hours whizzing by so quickly. If we didn't have such crazy schedules for the next few days, I can't think of anything I'd rather do than to curl up in front of the fire with you. But you've got an appointment downtown fairly early, and I've got to figure out if there is anything to save at GSS."

I reach for her hand and gently pull her toward me. She does not resist. I wrap my arms around her. As stupid as this might sound, all I want is to hug her.

An hour or so with Kristen in my arms would have been an ideal end to the evening, so the minute or so she remains next to me is great. Simultaneously, we gently pull away from one another. "I'll call you after my meeting with Mays."

"Please."

We kiss slowly and gently and without any sense of desperation.

"Drive carefully." She watches me open the front door.

I turn and head down the driveway.

CHAPTER TWENTY

I feel like a lemming following all the other lemmings into Boston on the Mass. Pike. Why did I ever agree to meet Deputy Director Mays at eight-thirty, at the height of the rush hour? I wonder if I should just head into the Post Office Square parking garage instead of searching for a parking space. Why not? I'll submit the receipt to Capital Investments and not worry about it. When you are sitting in bumper-to-bumper traffic, there is not a lot else to do except figure out your expense account. What about the muffins yesterday morning? Nah, that seems a bit cheap. Dinner in the North End? We did talk about business, although not too much. But the parking ticket, that's definitely going to be submitted.

I can't count how many times I've made this commute. At least I have the foresight to leave an extra half-hour for the inevitable traffic jam. Even so, I'm going to be late, albeit only about fifteen minutes. After the Allston-Cambridge tolls and four quarters, traffic starts to move at almost twenty miles per hour. At the end of the Mass. Pike, all traffic is literally shoveled onto a series of poorly marked ramps — designed to *help* the average driver get around and through Boston's roadways. Small wonder road rage is so prevalent.

Bobbing and weaving in the Financial District, I slide into a parking place on the sixth floor of the Post Office Square garage — that's six stories underground. The top of the garage is a very nice park, and everything else is below ground. If you are claustrophobic, I do not recommend parking in a fifty-foot-deep hole. However, with all respect to the builders and designers of the garage, it is well-lit, clean, and has classical music playing throughout, clearly a veiled attempt to soothe the aforementioned road rage. Each floor is designated by a flower: rose, iris, daffodil. I park on Sunflower and enter the elevator for a quick trip to the surface.

Once outside, I cross the park, now rather brown, toward the old Federal Building. The new Federal Building in which the courts and most offices are located has gone upscale on the waterfront. Needless to say, entering the building is something of an ordeal. Everyone and everything is searched. I mean everyone. I recognize one of the senior judges, who must have an office in the old building where he can escape from sniveling young law students.

Even though he knows each security guard by name, nonetheless, his briefcase is opened and he is required to pass through the metal detector. I don't mind security. It's better than the alternative. What I mind is special treatment for some folks. I think the notion that a lawyer who flashes an ID card is less likely to blow up a building than anyone else, is preposterous. Now, no more plastic IDs. Everyone goes through the search process.

Since I haven't brought anything with me to examine, I place my keys and remaining quarters into a clear plastic tray and pass through the detector without incident. As I approach the large directory at the far end of the building, since I have no idea where I'm going, the ubiquitous Agent Fitzgerald suddenly appears.

"Please follow me, Mr. Blackman." His voice is devoid of emotion. I am tempted to pinch him to see if he's real, but I resist. I can be a big boy when I try.

I follow Agent Fitzgerald down a hall toward what appears to be a service elevator. Makes sense. No it doesn't. What's wrong with the regular elevator? Now I am really nervous. Agent Fitzgerald ushers me inside, follows, and pushes 13. I know I'm deep in trouble. The regular elevators do not have a thirteenth floor button. What's on the thirteenth floor? I remind myself to count the floors from outside the building when — if I ever get out.

The door opens onto an opulent floor — by government standards. The walls are painted off-white, rather than pea green. Massive portraits of robed, stern-looking men adorn the walls. Oriental rugs cover the marble floors.

None of the doors bears either the number of the room or the name of the occupant. Clearly, if you didn't know where you were going, you had better not be there. About halfway down the corridor, we stop. Agent Fitzgerald knocks. The unmistakable voice of the deputy director booms out, "Stephen, please come in."

The door opens. How'd he do that? We enter. Me first. I'm sure Agent Fitzgerald thinks I'm going to bolt and run. Not far from the truth. I am spooked out.

"Jack, two cups of tea, please." At least I now know that Agent Fitzgerald has a first name.

I half expect to find myself in some kind of chamber of horrors, with every form of torture device known to man. Instead, I find Deputy Director Mays seated in a leather reclining chair. The room is furnished in nineteenth-century oak. In fact, the entire room and its contents are oak: paneling, table, roll-top desk, chairs — everything, except the recliner.

"Please don't think it discourteous if I don't rise to shake your hand." Grinning, Mays motions me to a chair.

"Please, take a seat. The chair is more comfortable than it looks. Believe me, I've spent most of my life in chairs, and these big old chairs are really pleasant to sit in."

"I should have scheduled our meeting for a little later so that you didn't hit the worst of the traffic," Mays remarks apologetically.

I shrug. "It was therapeutic."

"I've been staying at the Langham across the street, so I didn't think about you having to drive in." The Langham is one of Boston's most expensive hotels. No wonder our taxes are so high.

Once again, it seems that my mind is an open book.

"In case you're wondering, the Bureau keeps a permanent room at the Langham. Small, lower floor, no view of the park."

I feel guilty for thinking bad thoughts.

Our tea arrives just in time.

"Your announcement yesterday about the Ebola was rather disturbing." Mays sips his tea.

Yeah, like the end of the world.

"We knew nothing about the loss...potential loss, because GSS never told anyone that they were using Ebola in research. Your friend Mr. Harris is understandably very upset about this problem. While the storage facility for the Ebola was compliant with the state of the art, failure to register must be viewed in the worst light. This revelation raises many perplexing questions. Was someone, or multiple someones, trying to hide something or someone?"

Deputy Director Mays is beginning to talk like I think. Scary.

"There is going to be accountability when all is said

and done. However, we have released Mr. Harris, for the time being."

Deputy Director Mays is not a happy camper and I imagine that Ed isn't either. Simultaneously, we reach for our teacups.

"I'm sure you want a hundred questions answered, and although you're technically on a need-to-know basis, it's my opinion that you need to know everything."

What I really want to know is why is the FBI involved, especially if they really didn't know about the Ebola? And why do I need to know everything, when all I want is to know nothing? I hate that phrase — *need-to-know*.

"I'm sure you're still wondering what I was doing in Concord."

I'm going to get a facial. Maybe the wrinkles on my forehead spell out what's in my brain.

"Well, now that you mention it, the thought has crossed my mind." Yeah, like about a million times.

"Everything and everybody is getting checked out just a bit more closely, especially when potentially breakthrough scientific research is being done under the eyes of a former or not-so-former Israeli operative."

"Shit! Kettleman!" I mutter, hoping Mays doesn't hear.

"I think the Ebola is not central to whatever happened, unless..."

I'm feeling less comfortable by the second. "If the Ebola isn't central, why is Kettleman being watched?"

"Precaution."

"Mr. Mays, are you telling me that the FBI is routinely watching people without any evidence that they are engaged in an activity that might be illegal?"

"We cannot be too careful."

How can I tell the deputy director of the FBI that

spying on someone who's done nothing wrong, who doesn't associate with people who have done anything wrong, who doesn't have any known terrorist ties, and who has served in the military of a country who we consider in the family of allies, may be a violation of constitutional rights? So what else is new? While I would rather be safe than sorry, and we can't be caught asleep again, the other extreme isn't too pleasant either. New times — new rules. It doesn't mean I've got to like it. "If the Ebola isn't central, and the Bureau didn't even know about it and even if Kettleman was, is, in some way in the employ of the Israeli government, so what?"

Mays seems distracted. "We must treat the fact that the Ebola may not be in a safe place as a problem of the greatest magnitude."

Okay, so the FBI watches foreign nationals, especially those with ties, present or former, to their country of origin...sometimes. Israel is our friend, right? If Kettleman had been working at Midas Muffler, would he achieve *we're watching you* status? I wonder if Kettleman is an American citizen.

"Mr. Mays, please slow down. If the Ebola isn't central, what's the big deal about Kettleman? How does Gordon's death figure in? Why assume the Ebola is not the target and why assume it is not, at least for right now, in a safe place?"

"We have no doubt that Kettleman's association with GSS was not accidental. By having access to top-of-the-line research, an operative can feed information back to scientists in Israel working on similar projects. It's corporate espionage at its most sophisticated level."

"I agree. Then it simply becomes a matter of money and power. He who has a vaccine for cancer is likely to reap huge rewards. But the same thing is true whether the competition is Israeli or another American company. It wouldn't be the first time people have tried to steal corporate secrets for money. But why kill one of the keys to the development of the vaccine? The Ebola is the wild card."

"Well put, but it doesn't change the facts."

"Of course it does." I'm getting a little heated. "If the Ebola, rather than the vaccine, is the main issue, then the matter is not one of money or who has the cure for cancer. The issue radically changes."

"Are you so sure these are mutually exclusive?" The deputy director's voice is even louder than mine. "If the Israelis have a vaccine against Ebola, and presumably other biological diseases, they have effectively disarmed that threat from the arsenal of their enemies." Mays leans forward. "If the Israelis have an Ebola vaccine, they can use the Ebola against their neighbors in the name of national security."

"That's outrageous!" My voice is so loud that the door opens behind me and Agent Fitzgerald enters.

"Everything is fine." The deputy director leans back in his seat. "We're simply having a political discussion and we each are passionate about our positions." He grins at the retreating Fitzgerald, who closes the door behind him.

I'm reminded of my third-grade teacher, Miss Heinz. Whenever things got a bit heated, like loud, we were all required to take a *time out*.

"I'm sure the FBI has much more information than I do." I look straight at Mays. "But don't tell me that the government of Israel doesn't have access to almost every kind of biological substance known, whether benign or malevolent, including Ebola. I do not believe for one minute that Israel would ever participate in a first-strike biological attack. The reason no nation has attacked Israel is its massive arsenal of weapons of destruction, mass or otherwise. It's the same theory as the cold war."

"You are passionate, Stephen, but a bit misguided."

Mays points his finger at me. "If faced with a worldwide terrorist Jihad, a holy war, all the implications of which we are already witnessing, Israel would use anything and everything in that arsenal to defend itself, including biological warfare, provided it could protect its own citizens from its effects. And your cold war analogy doesn't hold up when people are prepared to die for their cause. It's because neither the Russians nor we were suicidal that the mutual deterrent theory worked."

He's right, damn it all, even though I may not want to hear it. Time to wake up. All my life, I have believed that there is a standard of civilized behavior, and now I am being dragged kicking and screaming into the ugly reality that certain people are so barbaric as to forfeit their rights to be a part of humankind.

There is still a large part of the picture I'm missing. Okay, the FBI watches GSS because of Kettleman, but it doesn't know about the Ebola. Why were they really watching him? Because they thought he might steal the cancer cure? Maybe, but that doesn't explain the agent planted inside GSS, who must have known about the special room in which the Ebola was stored. Either Mays is playing me for a fool or I am overestimating the competency of the FBI. Scary on both counts. It doesn't change one thing, there is one murder so far and two people are missing, presumed…dead or kidnapped, along with their years of critical research and, of course, the Ebola.

What am I doing here, other than to amuse William Howard Mays? I hope this is a bad dream and I am going to wake up…real soon. I look across the desk at a man who holds either all the answers or as few as I hold. I sure hope it's the former, since the latter is a glass more than half-empty.

"Plain and simple, we have a serious problem and we're prepared to use all our assets to resolve that problem.

And you're one of those assets. I don't know if you can be of any help, but I'm convinced, more than ever, that you're willing to do whatever you can."

I nod.

"Quite frankly, I don't know exactly what you can do. Ask questions of yourself and others. Pose scenarios and then punch holes in your assumptions. The puzzle pieces are well-hidden, but my gut instinct tells me that the answer to their location lies in plain sight. We're just not looking in the right places. You bring a different perspective, and that perspective is what I'm counting on."

I just listen, hearing nothing of substance but sensing that I'm being prepared to ride into the Valley of Death with the six hundred for this guy. I have no idea where to start. I keep feeling that somehow the deputy director and I are not on the same page of the script. "Since I don't have anything to offer you at the moment, I'm probably just taking up space." I'm still having a hard time reconciling the Ebola *disappearance* as a coincidence. Should I tell him that I think he is being less than candid with me? I begin to rise.

"Specifically..."

My ears begin to perk up.

"I want you to talk with the GSS people, especially the investor group. Ed Harris won't talk to me without a truckload of lawyers, so that's a dead end for now."

Can you really blame him? "And Miss Marks?"

"I think she'll assist you in any way she can, although I don't think she knows anything more than she's already told us. Keep in touch daily. Fitzgerald will give you a cell number where I can be reached."

Interview over, I know no more now than I did two hours ago. Time flies when you're having fun. Maybe I'll go home and watch some mindless reruns.

Now I'm flirting with escapism. I have no idea what

to do or what the real purpose of the meeting with the deputy director was. I can feel the hairs on the back of my neck rise ever so slightly. Not a good sign. I think I'll call Ed and set up a time for us to chat. Also Robert, and definitely Kristen — later. Around dinnertime.

I no sooner offer my hand to Mays, which he graciously shakes, than Fitzgerald suddenly appears from behind a closed door and announces, "I'll see you out."

Once again, I consider whether the room is bugged. The deputy director probably has a button under the edge of his desk with which to summon his minions, or is Fitzgerald instinctively tuned into his boss. I shudder to think.

I bid good-bye, follow Fitzgerald out, and find myself back on the street, holding a plain business card upon which a number is written. Mays's cell number, no doubt. How did Agent Fitzgerald manage to get the card in my hand without me even knowing? I'm completely out of it.

It's still a rather pleasant day and I'm hungry, not to mention tired, frustrated and scared.

Maybe I'll leave my car and stroll the few extra blocks to pay Ed and maybe Henry a surprise visit. I'll even ask them to lunch. An appealing subject. We can discuss how this whole scenario isn't holding water.

CHAPTER TWENTY-ONE

It's usually a quick walk to the offices of Capital Investments, but today it takes longer than it should. Partially because I'm oblivious to anything and anybody around me. I enter the elevator and automatically push 44.

"Steve…" I hear a voice behind me. Trying to appear reasonably coherent, I turn around and see a guy, about my age, who looks somewhat familiar. Focus, Stephen. Got it.

"Marty!" I almost shout, proud of my ability to lift the mental fog so quickly. "How the heck are you?" Remember, it's not polite to swear in an elevator.

"Between good and better." Marty, who has been in PR entirely too long, never answers a question. "And you?"

"Things are really great," I lie. Well, if meeting an apparently perfect woman on the eve of the destruction of the world is great, so be it.

The elevator reaches Marty's floor before we can continue this inane attempt at conversation.

"I'm still in Cambridge," he says. "Give me a call and we'll have a drink at the Plough & Stars."

I smile and nod as the doors close. Marty is a good guy, but he's never seemed to catch any breaks. Here I am feeling sorry for somebody else, who by his own admission is *between good and better*. Than what?

Forty-fourth floor, and again I have to deal with the Guardians of the Gate. As I approach the reception area, one of the twosome states, as matter-of-factly as you please, "Mr. Blackman, Mr. Harris will be out to see you in just a moment."

How the hell does she know whom I want to see and, why is Ed Harris waiting for my arrival? I'm not on an elevator, so it was okay to swear, if only to myself. Could the deputy director have called and foretold of my arrival? Why would he ever do that?

I don't get another second to contemplate. The door to the inner sanctum opens, and Ed welcomes me as if I'm his long-lost brother. "Stephen, I'm glad you're here. We need to talk."

So now it's Stephen instead of Steve.

"You bet your ass we gotta talk."

I follow Ed, not to the great space-center conference room, but to his corner office, furnished exactly as you would imagine: mahogany, leather, a small wet bar with what appears to be a genuine Revere silver tea service, and yes — even an antique telescope to watch the comings and goings in Boston Harbor.

Ed gestures toward a chair to which a few cows have donated their hides. I slide into its recesses.

"Can I offer you something?"

Gracious to the core. "Coke, root beer, anything carbonated, non-diet, and cold." I guess lunch is going to wait.

How am I going to subtly ask Ed why he is waiting for me?

Ed hands me a glass with several ice cubes and a bottle of Coke. His hands are trembling. Ever see a guy who is ready to explode if he keeps whatever is bothering him inside for one more second? That's Ed.

Before he spills the beans, I have to warn him that not only is our conversation not privileged, but I probably have an obligation to report everything to Mr. Mays.

"Ed, before we talk, I think you should make sure that it's okay with your attorneys."

"I know about your meeting with Deputy Director Mays."

"How?" I'm getting paranoid, and more than a little upset that my activities are becoming general knowledge.

"He told me yesterday at the Colonial that he planned to meet with you this morning, and that he was going to ask you to continue your investigation, and I should cooperate with you. That's why I figured that after you were done with him, you'd come over here."

Does everybody know what I'm going to do before I do it?

"I really need to talk with you, and I'm going to leave it up to you how much to disclose, and to whom." Ed is squirming like a little kid who has to go to the bathroom.

"Are you sure you want to do this?"

"I don't have a choice."

"Yes you do."

"I do not!" His voice is firm and seems to lower an octave.

Shit! What is going on?

"Deputy Director Mays didn't know about the Ebola because he wasn't supposed to!"

Leaping hardly describes my next movement.

Within the blink of an eye, I'm toe-to-toe with Ed Harris. He jumps back, but only for the second he needs to regain his composure.

"Stephen, please sit down!"

I do. Why? I don't know. I should walk out. I don't think I'm going to like what I'm about to hear.

"Bioterrorism has always been a concern of our civilian and military agencies. Now, more than ever, the need to prepare for and the ability to defend against, these horrors is a top priority." Ed slowly paces across the carpeted floor, more like a professor than someone who is withholding information from the FBI.

"There are numerous agencies at various levels, each theoretically cooperating with one another to coordinate this effort. This has not always been the case. Our intelligence organizations have treated each other on a need-to-know basis. The problem is, who determines who needs to know what. Although strides have been made, old habits are hard to break."

I'm not hearing anything new. A lack of information-sharing has already led to unspeakable consequences, but it's being remedied. Where is Ed going with this?

"GSS was under contract to produce an anti-Ebola vaccine," he continues. "This research was to be conducted in absolute secrecy, and carried out in parallel with our regular research. Only Onellon and Gordon were to participate in the work, and all results were to be kept by them personally. A rather elaborate encryption system for their notes was implemented."

"What was Kettleman's role?"

"He was to coordinate the efforts of all their research with the research of other groups. Kettleman also acts as the CFO of the company and does the daily work of running GSS, which he does very well. The company continued uninterrupted in its primary research, but the Ebola project began to take on certain urgencies, and both Gordon and Onellon were spending a significant portion of their time and energies on the vaccine."

I wonder if Ed knows that the FBI has figured out that Kettleman is an Israeli agent.

"I was briefed along with Colonel Galjarian at least weekly."

Colonel Galjarian? Christ, I am so far over my head that I feel short of breath, like a man who's fallen overboard. I'm getting too old for this kind of crap.

"It seemed as if the whiz kids were within days of producing a vaccine for advanced mammal testing. Now they're gone, their research is gone and the Ebola is gone."

"That's it? You're telling me there was Ebola and now it's gone?" I'm not trying to be cute, I'm incredulous. How could this group of reasonably bright, which may be subject to debate, people lie to me about the Ebola? There are so many holes in this story, you'd need an army of dentists to fill them. "Ed, I think you should have a serious talk with Deputy Director Mays." I try to remain calm although I'm so angry that I want to strangle Ed, maybe Henry, certainly the *Colonel*, and hopefully not Kristen.

I want to know what's going on, but my intuition tells me something different. Maybe I should follow Mays' advice, try to get Ed to fill in the blanks and then report to him. I really wish I'd been out of town when he called. I am caught in a web, plain and simple, and it looks like I'm lunch. Speaking of lunch, I've lost my appetite.

"May I ask a couple of questions?" I feel surprising calm.

"Why, of course." Ed has just confessed that he withheld information during the course of an investigation. How illegal is that? But what is the FBI really investigating, if they didn't even know about the Ebola and if the murder of Gordon was a local matter? Kettleman? Nothing fits.

"I'm getting hungry." Ed sounds tired. "Another sandwich from the *Hole in the Wall*?"

He sure knows how to hurt a guy.

"Sure, roast beef on an onion roll with lettuce, tomato, and mayo."

Ed calls in my roast beef and a BLT for himself, with extra chips. I do not have a very good feeling about this entire situation…except about Kristen. Shit, if it's Colonel Galjarian, what if it's Major Marks? I smell a conspiracy. Come to think of it, Ed didn't say that Robert was a member of *our* Armed Forces, now did he?

A few minutes with a sandwich might give me time to add up the number of crimes that already have been committed.

It's hard to believe that I can't remember a single bite of that roast beef sandwich. I'm either too hungry or too preoccupied. Probably both. I'm not only on the horns of a dilemma, I'm being gored by them. To whom do I owe loyalty? Ed? As a friend or as my employer? Is Capital Investments my employer, or is it GSS? Time to start all over again.

I'm staring directly at Ed. "I detest bullshit."

"So do I, but sometimes things aren't what they seem."

This is beginning to sound a little too pat. I think I prefer being called Stephen.

"We need to start at the beginning, as if the briefing never took place, and you are going to tell me everything," I state.

Ed hesitates. "The fact that Gordon was apparently murdered changes a lot." He states this so matter-of-factly that it scares me.

I'm going to let the word *apparently* slip by, for now. I have never heard of a person shooting himself behind his own ear. "If you want my help, you're going to have to tell me everything, not just what you think I want to hear or need to know, but everything. And you are going to have to convince me, beyond a reasonable doubt, that you are telling me the truth. It's that simple."

Ed looks up. "That's fair, but not simple. While I have become privy to most of the really important information, things have changed during the last few weeks, and while I'm sure that what I know is accurate, I can't say with the highest level of certainty that I have all the pieces. Actually, I'm not sure that any one person has all the information necessary to satisfy your curiosity."

When in doubt, make a sentence as complicated as possible.

"You know, Ed, I can take a hike, submit a bill for two days' work, tell Mays what we've said, and feel that I've done as much as possible."

"That is simply not possible!"

"Why the hell not?" My voice is rising.

"Because, this thing is a whole lot bigger than you can possibly imagine.

"Try me. I have a great imagination. And based on what I've heard so far, there's not a lot that would really surprise me."

The veins on the back of Ed's neck are becoming more pronounced. This is getting too heated for comfort.

"Stephen, let's take a deep breath."

I thought Ed was the one hyperventilating. Me, I'm just pissed off and confused...in that order. "It's your show for the next half-hour. Then I'll decide what to do. Fair enough?"

He nods his affirmation. I return to my chair, and Ed to his desk.

"Almost three years ago," he starts, with a sigh, "I was introduced to Bob Galjarian at the home of a friend in New York. It was a purely social gathering. We talked about everything except business. He was very pleasant, and I rather enjoyed the evening. I asked my host about him the next day. I was told that he ran a small venture firm in D.C., was reputed to be a player in the biotech field who had invested in a number of rather successful projects, several of which I knew something about. I made a number of calls over the next couple of days, and everyone confirmed that Robert was just what he appeared to be — a smart, totally above-board guy, aggressive, yet attentive to details. And successful, of course. He seemed to have the inside track on any number of deals that would fit perfectly into our portfolio strategy."

Ed rises from his chair and begins pacing again. "Then several weeks later, I get a call from Robert at the office. He said he was going to be in Boston, and wondered if I would like to join him for lunch the following day. I agreed, and we met at Locke Ober's."

Locke Ober's is the place for power lunches. Until recently, it was strictly "men only." Fortunately that's changed — the part about "men only," not the part about power lunches.

Ed is not about to be stopped now that he's started. "We talked about portfolio strategy, investment opportunities, and the economy in general. He was very self-assured, and reflected an extensive technical knowledge. His demeanor was pleasant, but at the same time, he was also very intense. I was a little put off, actually. I enjoyed his lighter side and respected the depth of his familiarity with the world in which he was investing, but, there was something else."

I'm hoping Ed will at least stop to breathe.

"We left with the promise that if either of us ever came across a deal in which the other might want to participate, we would call. Two weeks later, I received an e-mail from Robert with a business plan attached — GSS. I began to read the plan. It really was very good. I sent out an interoffice e-mail asking if anyone had heard of any of the principals — Onellon, Gordon, or Kettleman. Within a matter of minutes, a young associate knocked on my door and suggested that I look at a document he was holding. It was an original copy of the GSS plan, which he said came into the office the day before and was assigned to him for first reading. Coincidental — yes, but suspicious, no."

He takes a deep breath. "Not yet. My first thought was that Robert and we had been sent the same plan, and he had simply read his first and was giving me the heads-up on a good deal."

So far, perfectly logical.

"I called to let him know that I had received a hard copy of the plan as well, and that I agreed that so far it looked good. Robert replied that a friend of his had also received a copy of the plan. To make a long story just a bit shorter, it appears six plans were sent out. Well, we all thought it was great, we all decided to invest, and Capital took the lead for basically two reasons: one, we had been looking for an investment and needed to fill a fund; and two, we were in the Boston area, the home of the principals. Due diligence performed, closed, and funded. No glitches, no problems. Everyone checked out, research continued, reports prepared, everything was fine.

"Then, about six months after the closing, I get a call from Robert asking if I would come to Washington to discuss GSS, as well as several other projects he was working on. He apologized for being unable to meet in Boston, something to do with his schedule, but he assured me that if I could take the morning shuttle, he'd pick me up and I'd be home for dinner. We made an appointment for the following Monday.

In retrospect, he seemed a bit anxious and concerned that we couldn't meet earlier."

I'm starting to wonder where all this is going. Nowhere good, I'm sure.

"When I landed at Reagan National, I was met by a uniformed driver in the terminal, holding a card with my name on it. I just assumed that Robert had sent a driver to take me to his office. As I approached the driver, Robert literally appears out of nowhere and greets me like a long-lost brother. We follow the driver to a car parked next to the curb. Even before 9/11, no one ever left a car unattended at the curb. The car was a basic dark gray Crown Victoria with… government plates."

I sense that Ed is beginning to tell me even more than I want to know. If Galjarian is somehow affiliated with the government, why doesn't Ed want Mays in the loop? I glance at my watch. His half-hour is up — but I'm not going to tell him that just yet.

"We drove to the Pentagon. The bloody Pentagon. We're waved through security. Can you imagine? We were waved through security!"

I can't tell if Ed was impressed or depressed by the fact. I admit that getting near the Pentagon as a civilian, let alone inside, is big-time.

"To make a long story short…"

"Don't worry about my time, Ed. I can decide for myself what's important."

He sighs. "We were met by three men in their late fifties — two generals and a navy vice admiral, and were told that we are expected in conference room 53A immediately. Conference rooms in the Pentagon are designated by floor and then ring and then side of building. So we start to quickstep to the elevator. Two marines fall in behind us. Stephen, believe me, I didn't have the foggiest idea what was going on. It is very obvious that Robert was getting preferential treatment. We crossed to the center ring and entered conference room A, which faces conference room B in the fourth ring."

I guess these guys don't spend a lot of time gazing out their windows while working. One part of me really wants to know where this is going. The other part wants to crawl under my covers and sleep 'til spring.

"We are met by four more men, each in civilian clothing, and two women, each a two-star general. I cannot adequately express the feeling I felt deep in the pit of my stomach."

Suddenly the phone rings. I jump. It's like being abruptly awakened from a deep sleep.

As Ed reaches for the phone, he mutters to no one in particular, "I left explicit instructions that I was not to be interrupted.

"Yes?" Ed's voice is edgy. He listens intently, nods a few times, and says, "I guess I don't have a choice. Please bring them down to my office." He hangs up the phone, turns to me, and remarks with an ironic smile, "Speak of the devil. It's Robert Galjarian, and another man whom he did not introduce to the receptionist."

Now I'm feeling that same feeling in the pit of my stomach that Ed couldn't describe. I wonder if breaking into tears will help.

Less than a heartbeat later, Ed's office door opens and in walks Robert Galjarian, together with the other man, who looks like GI Joe in civvies. I can't believe my eyes. Colonel Robert Galjarian looks like he's just stepped out of a fashion ad — tailored Brooks Brothers suit, blue shirt with a white collar, and a tie that matches his pocket handkerchief. Whatever happened to the old, rumpled Robert Galjarian? I think I liked him better.

"Glad you're here, Stephen. Please sit down, Ed." He

makes no attempt to introduce his companion. He merely slides into a chair and addresses Ed, "Did you have a chance to brief him?"

"I was in the process of doing so when you unexpectedly arrived."

"I thought I left you a message that I'd be here today. Sorry. No harm, no foul. Now we can get down to brass tacks."

So many clichés, so little time.

"Stephen," Galjarian begins, "I'm a senior member of a group whose sole responsibility is to coordinate the efforts of various civilian and military agencies in gathering information about groups that might pose a threat to our country. I report only to the director of homeland security and to the president. I try to make sure that information is shared between the various organizations. Unfortunately that's not always possible, and this may be one of those situations. We are not only dealing with a killer virus strain from hell, but also the vaccine. I've seen how much panic a few letters with anthrax can cause. The operations of the government are disrupted. This is more serious for two reasons. First, the bug itself and the murder of one of its handlers. And second, maybe more importantly, we believe this to be an internal problem."

"Internal?" I hesitate. "What do you mean?"

"Remember how everybody thought that Oklahoma City was external and how we all jumped to the wrong conclusions? Then 9/11 — external. Boston Marathon — external or internal? We can't make assumptions."

"I'm more than somewhat concerned that a simple private detective is involved in a series of events vastly beyond anything for which he's been trained." I hate talking about myself in the third person, but at least I've made myself clear. It's incredibly frustrating that Galjarian can be so matter-of-fact while I'm on the verge of a breakdown.

"You're here for several reasons," Galjarian says. "You are smart, you have a perspective which is not tainted by years of trying to second-guess someone willing to blow himself to kingdom come for a cause, and you seem to be in everyone's confidence."

"Does that include Deputy Director Mays?"

"You bet your ass it does, but it also includes my confidence, which is a lot harder to get. And, I might add, the confidence of Ed and Henry and of course the lovely Ms. Marks."

Am I being complimented or conned?

I sigh. "What can I do?"

"Other than finding the Ebola, the vaccine, the murderer, Kettleman, Onellon, and the group behind the entire plan, try listening."

This guy is really pissing me off, although he seems to have just the hint of a smile on his face.

"Stephen, we can't trust the FBI on this one!"

And they're supposed to be the good guys. Galjarian doesn't hold back any punches.

"The operation was simple: develop a vaccine under the guise of a respectable business. And it was working. Then something happened. The FBI planted one of their own in GSS without anyone knowing. Gave him a stutter and got him access to the Concord house on the ruse that he was a handyman. Six weeks later, the whole thing blows up. Now, I need to know exactly what you and the deputy director have talked about."

"May I ask a simple question?" I interrupt.

Everyone nods.

"How do I know you guys are wearing the white hats and not Mr. Mays?"

"Fair question," he replies. "Call this number and

satisfy yourself. If you're still suspicious because you've watched too many movies about spies and technology, I propose that we all go to Hanscom Field, hop in my plane, and fly to Andrews Air Force Base right now. We can go to the Pentagon or the White House, or both, for that matter."

"Okay," I reply. "Let's go."

Without blinking, Galjarian reaches across to Ed's phone, punches in some numbers, and says, "Be ready to go in twenty minutes. Andrews. Car to 1600." Turning to me, he adds, "Let's go. We can talk on the way. Ed, do you want to meet the president, too?"

Ed lifts his eyebrows. "Remember, I've already had a briefing, so I'm more comfortable with you than Stephen is."

I don't know how far to push. I rise to leave, saying, "I'll follow you in my car so that when I return, you don't have to worry about ground transportation."

"We'll all go in my car. It'll give us more time to talk. We'll all be returning to Boston later today anyway." I guess I just got told off.

I'm beginning to think that I should fold this hand and ask for a rain check. But maybe that's what Galjarian is doing…brinksmanship. It would be cool to go to the White House, but do I really have time with mankind hanging in the balance?

"Maybe later. You've made your point."

He smiles again.

"Stephen, it really doesn't bother me. It shows good judgment on your part. The stakes are high, and you need to know who's covering your backside."

"I trust Ed and he trusts you. That's good enough. Except I need to know, can I trust Ms. Marks? Is she what she seems, or is she some kind of operative?"

"You also show good taste and good sense. She is exactly what she says, a professional interim CEO. We have used her in several other situations where we needed a temp. She's good and smart, but doesn't quite know everything."

"What's everything?"

"Specifically, that I am any different from what I appear to be — a businessman with a problem. We've spent years developing this cover, and it's worked. We've also made a lot of money. Well, the government has made money from our investments. When I retire, maybe I'll do this for real. I'm actually quite good, but I've also got one hell of a research department and enough deep pockets to weather any storm." He starts to chuckle.

"Another question?"

He nods.

"Kettleman. What's his role?"

"Why do you ask?" Robert rubs his nose.

"Mays thinks he's an Israeli operative, and that this entire situation may be orchestrated to get the Ebola and vaccine into the control of Israel as some kind of deterrent or maybe even offensive weapon."

Robert smiles. "Stephen, you've just given us a very valuable piece of information."

"You mean about Kettleman?"

"About what's happening inside the FBI. Kettleman and I have been associated for many years. He's dedicated and loyal. We choreographed his association with the Israeli government. Bottom line, he's a double agent."

That's so Ian Fleming.

"The thought of him disrupting the research and testing of the vaccine is ridiculous. With the vaccine, not only is Ebola as a terrorist weapon neutralized, but also bioterrorism itself is virtually eliminated. Israel would be a direct beneficiary. I can't figure out the FBI, unless they are trying to disseminate misinformation." Galjarian strokes his chin.

"Mays' theory is that if Israel could control both the Ebola and the vaccine, then they would not only be able to deter the use by terrorists, but if backed against the wall, use it offensively, protecting their own citizenry."

"Stephen, in the last ten minutes, you've been more helpful in explaining the actions of the FBI than you can imagine."

"Okay, let's make a deal, you fill me in and I'll give you all the tidbits of information I've collected, which would be less random if I knew what the hell was going on."

The colonel nods. "Reasonable, provided you agree that you won't go back to Mays unless instructed to do so, and not discuss anything we say with anyone. Otherwise, we will simply have to kill you."

I don't share the humor.

"What about Ms. Marks?"

"You'll continue to feed her information and generally discuss the investigation. Otherwise she'll become suspicious, and might take those suspicions to the wrong people. We'll tell you what to tell her."

"And Mays?"

"Deputy Director William Howard Mays. Now he's both the problem and the cure."

How can a man who has served his nation for three decades and overcome the obstacles of disability and race to rise to the top, be both a problem and a cure?

"If you think I didn't understand you before, that last comment doesn't make any sense at all."

"Mr. Mays is a wonderful public servant. He has a keen mind, but also, unfortunately, a very trusting disposition. His staff is fiercely loyal to him and he to them. He basically runs the Bureau. However, his sense of loyalty has gone too far. He never wants to hear anything bad about his agency. We believe that for several years, there has been at least one, maybe as many as three, people in the Bureau with access to a lot of important information, whose true loyalty is suspect. Mays won't believe any of it, even when confronted with evidence that there is a breach of security close to the top. We have planted sensitive, but false information, at various levels of the FBI, and found it leaking out the back. Mays blamed the leak on everyone, except the Bureau, citing safeguard upon safeguard that makes it impossible. Stephen, the deputy director is truly a good guy with a fatal flaw — he cannot or will not accept the fact that there is always a bad apple in every barrel."

I'm exhausted. I've been taught to believe that the FBI was an organization filled with Eliot Ness types — incorruptible, All-American with crew cuts. Well, if you stop and think about it, the agency was founded by J. Edgar Hoover. Need I say more about the former director? International intelligence groups have tried for years, with varying degrees of success, to infiltrate each other's inner circles. Why not a domestic organization? With agencies more open to each other, getting well-situated in the FBI would get you, albeit through the back door, into the international information arena. But what about the comment that this caper might be internal? "If I'm to believe you, then what's to prevent the individual or individuals inside the FBI from planting misinformation to throw everyone off the track in an investigation?"

"You mean like shooting Gordon gangland style?"

"Point made. But although there may be a mole, who's to say the entire scenario isn't being orchestrated from an external source?"

"Counterpoint." Galjarian nods. "This is exactly why you are on board. We've assumed that the problem is internal, because there's a flaw inside the FBI. Someone whose political views have gotten pushed off the chart. It really never occurred to us that the mole could have been hired by an external source. Maybe Mays is aware of the leak, and even knows his identity, which would explain the Kettleman-Israeli connection."

The wheels are spinning a million miles an hour in Galjarian's head. I swear I hear a whirring sound.

I never know when to keep my mouth shut. "Maybe we should take the deputy director into our confidence. Maybe he knows something about Kettleman that you don't. Maybe…he's right."

You can hear a pin drop on the nice antique Oriental rug.

Galjarian is ashen. It had never remotely occurred to him that he might not be a hundred percent right. I'm re- minded of the onion analogy — the more you peel an onion, the smaller it becomes, until finally you are left with nothing. The artichoke, on the other hand, represents quite the opposite. The more you peel, the closer you get to the heart. I hope we're in the artichoke section of the market.

"If you really want my opinion…" I look around the room, unsure whether or not anyone wants my opinion. "Let's simplify what we know and how we know it by putting everything on a single piece of paper. It sounds simplistic, but I'm the kind of guy who needs to visualize things."

Maybe everyone in the spy business is so paranoid that the thought of putting anything in writing makes them freeze.

"That might not be a bad idea." Robert Galjarian reenters the world of the living.

We spend the next hour creating a series of charts by subject, by person, and by time. We use a lot more than one piece of paper, so all of our drafts, doodles and notes are dropped into a single shredder wastepaper basket. No sense in being careless.

Three issues loom large: Kettleman, friend or foe; the fact that the FBI seems to be carrying on an independent operation; and the murder of Gordon. There are still many unresolved questions, like who, why, how, and where; but the consensus is that we need to answer the Kettleman and FBI issues at the very least.

I can offer little to help solve the riddle. I have no opinion of Kettleman, except that two major people in our government hold opposite opinions of the man and only one of those opinions can be correct.

Figuring out the FBI's agenda is not going to get done by the four of us sitting in a room. Back to zero. Maybe I should beg my leave. I glance down at my watch and gasp. It's almost six o'clock. I have a gnawing feeling that we are overlooking something obvious. Maybe I'm just getting hungry. Yet again, I rise from my chair and announce that I've had enough.

Galjarian stops me. "I'm sorry to ask this, but could you get in touch with Kristen and tell her that you spent the entire day with Mays? You know, going over files and discussing possibilities. If she asks, tell her that you have more questions than answers, but that you're scheduled to come up tomorrow and talk with Ed and me. Act discouraged and frustrated, but do not go into details."

Acting discouraged and frustrated will be easy. Getting in touch with Kristen might not be.

"Do you think all of us meeting tomorrow would be productive?" I look across at Galjarian.

No one is quick to answer.

"I think we've made a lot of progress." He tugs his ear. "It's like a jigsaw puzzle, and we were able to fit several key pieces together today. A little time to digest is probably a good thing. Let's get together here around ten tomorrow morning. You can avoid the traffic."

Nodding, I walk to the door and begin to retrace my steps toward the reception area. I glance over my shoulder and see Ed looking up at the ceiling in silence. The thought of Kristen suddenly floods my senses. I'll call her from the lobby, rather than use my cell phone. Paranoia or caution, I wonder.

CHAPTER TWENTY-TWO

The doors of the elevator open to the still-bustling lobby — and the pay phone has a line. I thought everyone had a cell phone nowadays. Forget it. I'll call from the car after all. It's already dark. I get so depressed when the days get shorter. No wonder there are so many suicides in Sweden. I enter the parking garage and suddenly remember that the payment routine is backwards. You have to stand in line and pay the cashier, who gives you a receipt that you give to the machine on your way out. If this is intended to speed my exit, it's a fiction. All it does is change the place where you wait — in the lobby versus your car.

Ten minutes later, I descend to the Sunflower parking level. As I approach my car, I notice a white piece of paper on the windshield, held in place by the wiper blade. An ad for a great new restaurant? A flyer for the newest shoe repair *while-u-wait*? Whatever it is, I instinctively look for a trash barrel. As I reach the car and remove the offending piece of paper, however, I see that it's a handwritten note or rather hand-printed, in what appears to be crayon.

It is critical that we meet.
I need to trust you.

My heart rate goes off the charts. Is this some kind of sick joke? But who or why? I grip the corner of the paper. I want to be careful in the event there are fingerprints. Come to think about it, I don't know if fingerprints show up on paper. I must have missed that lecture at detective school. Where do I take the document and get the fingerprints lifted or identified? Whoever wrote this apparently wants to trust me, and I don't even know whom to trust myself. Suddenly I freeze. Maybe the writer is watching me at this moment, and I need to give him some kind of signal. I open the car door and carefully put the paper in the passenger's seat. I get back out and look around as inconspicuously as possible in a garage full of cars. Now what? For no reason in particular, I open the trunk of my car and start to rearrange the contents. I make no effort to peer around the trunk's lid. If I'm being watched, I want to give the watcher an opportunity to do whatever he or she intends to do. After about five minutes that seems like an hour, I emerge from the darkened hole in which I've been fumbling with a winter scarf. Okay, it's the only thing I can think about grabbing. I walk around the car. What do I expect to find anyway? Another note?

There it is, under the wiper blade again.

I can only pray I'm not having a heart attack, because my ticker's working overtime.

Should I grab the paper and jump into the car or try looking around and see if I can ID someone? There are only about 700 cars on this floor, so who am I kidding about seeing someone who obviously doesn't want to be seen?

There's a second message tempting me to do something. I quickly move toward the front of the car, gingerly take the paper by a corner, return to the driver's-side door, and slide in behind the wheel. Sweat is pouring down my face, despite the temperature being forty degrees.

Tomorrow, noon, between Fanueil Hall and Quincy Market.

I place the second paper on top of the first. My head is spinning. Hoax or reality? Is this an effort by Mays to see how I'll react? What if this is an attempt by the kidnappers to get me to go to one of the most public places in all of Boston for a meeting — maybe to hear the kidnappers' demands. Finally. I get out of the car and lock the door. I feel like throwing up. Rather than embarrass myself, I take the elevator up to the lobby again and enter the men's room. A splash of cold water is the best antidote, but for what? Pulling my thoughts together is getting increasingly difficult.

Who can I trust? Is this a trap? A test? A joke? How can I get out of tomorrow's meeting or leave if it gets too dangerous? Coward! You bet! Should I get the notes analyzed before I go to the meeting? By whom? What about backup? If it was written by someone involved in the disappearance, will this person bolt if he or she senses a setup?

Who can I trust? I'm repeating myself.

I think I'm going to scream. A perfectly mature and manly reaction.

What if Kristen isn't home tonight?

First things first. I walk over to the bank of pay phones, find one that hasn't been totally vandalized, and lift the receiver to call Kristen. Fifty cents! What a ripoff. I'm glad that I've got a lot quarters. I was angry when the cost went from ten cents to twenty-five, but fifty, that's robbery. No wonder everyone has a cell phone with a zillion free minutes. Being the passive soul that I am, I insert not one, but two quarters. One ring...two...three and then...the answering machine. Shit!

"Kristen, this is Stephen. Just finished an all-day marathon and wanted to see if you're free. I'm just leaving the Post Office Square garage. Try me on my cell or at home."

I'm devastated, although I keep hearing a little distant voice of warning.

Down six floors again. Once again I approach the Volvo. I immediately freeze. Shit! Another piece of paper on my windshield. Well, what was I expecting? Maybe someone broke into the car and is hiding in the back seat. Like that story about the woman and the axe murderer. I quicken my steps. Take the paper by the corner.

Opening Soon – Speedy Copy – your one stop for all your copying needs

I flip the paper over — blank. I almost crumple the paper in a combination of disgust and relief, but consider on second thought that I'll add it to the other two...just in case. Opening the Volvo's door, I automatically glance into the back seat. Nothing. Nobody.

I begin my ascent. Ten minutes later, I exit into a dark November Boston evening and head for the Mass. Pike, resigned to watching *CSI*. Like most Americans, I've been vacuumed into TV wasteland, reading less, watching more, and being entertained not at all. And this is one of the most popular show on television excluding *American Idol* and now *The Voice*, not Mays, which are each only on the air for a few months — thankfully.

Remind me to stop at Barnes and Noble.

As I wend my way along the edge of Chinatown,

the silence is shattered by the opening strains of Beethoven's Fifth — not from the radio, but from my cell phone. Hey, it's better than *YMCA*, which I recently heard coming from the cell phone of an elderly gentleman.

"Hello?"

"Stephen? Stephen? Are you there?"

"Hi, Kristen. Sorry, but there is a ton of traffic and my attention is being diverted by a delivery truck trying to pass another truck double parked on a street only wide enough for two cars. They're exchanging papers and saying something to each other, in some Asian tongue. I don't think they were exchanging pleasantries, however."

She laughs. I smile, although with altercations of the nature just described, I worry about someone pulling out a knife, or better yet a gun, and resolving the dispute on the spot.

I miss the Mass. Pike entrance. Wishful thinking, or am I going to hate myself because it will take me no less than twenty minutes to get back to the entrance?

"I got your message," Kristen says. "I'm free if you are. Why don't you come over for a drink, and then we can go into the Square and get something to eat?"

"Sounds great." I don't want to tell her that I just blew past the Pike entrance and am already halfway to her house. "I'll be there in about fifteen minutes."

"Take your time. I'm about to jump into the shower."

"No fair! You'll be clean and gorgeous and I'll be stinky and wrinkled."

There is a long pause.

"I've got plenty of clean towels."

I almost recite my *save water, take a shower with a friend* line, but refrain. "Leave me some hot water," is the best I can come up with.

"I'll put a Pinot Grigio on ice."

God, I wish I had used the *share-a-shower* line. "Bye."

"Drive carefully. See you soon." Her voice is very caring. It's been a long time since anyone sounded as if she really cares.

I glance down at the passenger's seat and see my anonymous letters. Reality sucks.

CHAPTER TWENTY-THREE

The drive is sporadically slow — as expected. That is probably the best way to describe Boston traffic. It means you can be driving at, say, forty miles per hour, and all of a sudden, the driver in front of you jams on his brakes in response to the car in front of him doing the same thing. You then proceed for about ten minutes at a stop-and-go pace until you get to what you think is the source of the problem, only to find nothing. That's right, traffic has gone into that insane seesaw drive for no reason at all. I think I'll call it the Bostonian two-step.

Driving on Storrow Drive, a divided road hugging the banks of the Charles River on the Boston side, is also a nightmare. Built after the Second World War, the road is one switchback after another. If I drive at thirty-five miles per hour, the drive is pleasant but challenging. At fifty-five, which everyone tries to do, it makes Daytona look safe. In theory, only passenger cars are permitted to travel the road, but pickup trucks and utility vans are common users as well. What makes Storrow Drive so exciting is right around Labor Day, and again around Memorial Day, when college students, primarily from Boston University, are moving in and out of their dorms. Invariably, a student in a U-Haul rent-a-truck decides to use Storrow Drive, without reading the signs that warn of "LOW CLEARANCE" every couple of hundred feet. Invariably, that student will crash into a bridge or tunnel, wedging himself in so tightly that the road closes down for hours at a time. You would think that by now, the word would have gotten out, but no.

I say all this by way of digression, since I really don't want to think about the myriad issues currently staring me in the face. Seeing Kristen will make me smile, but the prospect also makes me more than a little upset. I need to talk to somebody I can trust. As much as I would like to believe that Kristen is that person, I can't be too sure. Logic…instinct… logic…instinct. I'm not sure I'm up to the task. If these notes are genuine, it represents the first real break in the case. I can't check them out without trusting Robert Galjarian and his group or William Howard Mays and his group.

Okay. Assume they are genuine. I can't ask for help because it might scare away whoever is reaching out to me. Why me? Why is everyone so trusting of me when I'm not trusting of my own judgment most of the time? What if I'm walking into a trap and the bad guys, whoever they may be, want to torture me to find out what I know? Sounds too dramatic. Where does this leave me? Depressed.

Should I tell Kristen everything, even though I was asked, or rather instructed, not to? Is she really just a professional interim CEO, or does she work for more than one employer? Sometimes a glass of Pinot Grigio and a nice dinner are just the thing to make everything clear — clear as mud.

If you think Storrow Drive is bad, try crossing the river and driving into Harvard Square. Jaywalking developed into an art form in Cambridge. It is neither gender nor age biased. Everyone walks wherever and whenever he or she feels like it. Add in a couple of hundred bikes, buses, double-parked cars, and the occasional moving van, and a journey into the Square becomes a true adventure. Last time I went to Kristen's house, I came from North Cambridge. Last time? It was only last night! I'm losing all grasp of time.

If it wasn't for the fact that I'd lived in Harvard Square for so many years, I think the car might end up in Arlington or Watertown, or even worse...Somerville. As it is, however, I glide onto Frances Avenue and pull in behind Kristen's VW.

"Door's open!"

I can make out Kristen's silhouette moving away from the second-floor window. A smile flashes across my face. Who cares if she is a spy, anyway?

It suddenly occurs to me that I don't have any clean clothes into which I can change, unless I've left my tennis bag in the trunk. Then I'll have clean underwear, a sweater, and a white collared shirt. Unlike many of my friends, I always take my sports bag out of the car the same day I use it, put the clothes into the hamper, replace the dirty togs with a clean set, and replace the bag in the trunk. Am I anal or what? The problem usually arises *off season*, when I change tennis gear for foul-weather and then cold-weather clothing. When was the last time I played tennis, anyway?

Stop stalling and just look in the damn trunk, Stephen. I'm a bit nervous. Kristen has that effect on me. I need to talk over the day's events with someone; and even though I've been told not to let Kristen in on the details, it's essential that I get a second opinion. I surely don't have anyone else to turn to.

Slow down. You've known this woman only two

days. Well, two and a half and you're already up to your ass in alligators.

Shit. I slam the car door and head around to the trunk. Even though I've just spent the longest five minutes of my life staring into my trunk at the garage, I can't seem to recall its contents. I hesitate before opening the lid. What if there is a body in there? Dead or alive?

Now I'm just being stupid. I open the lid and gaze inside. I can't believe my eyes. Not only is my tennis bag resting comfortably inside, but so is a box of shirts I had just picked up from the dry cleaners — light starch.

Okay, how do I do this? Walk into Kristen's house with a box of shirts and essentially an overnight bag? I don't think so. Maybe just knock and walk in, casually saying *Hi, I'm here. Are you decent?* Dumb line. When she comes down, wait until she mentions something. Worst case, I go out to the car and get my stuff later. Much better.

"Stephen, are you lost?" Kristen calls from the front door.

Her voice startles me. I look up and, of course, bang my head on the trunk lid, but I refrain from uttering my customary curse. I just sheepishly turn toward the sound of her voice. No one can accuse this lady of tarrying. She is wearing slacks, a turtleneck, and a big, fuzzy sweater. Ready for dinner.

"Wine, shower, dinner...you pick the order." Her voice is soothing somehow, trying to be cool. Well, maybe not!

After much thought, I leave the bag, shrug, slam the trunk, which I know intentionally bangs me on my head, and walk toward Kristen. She greets me with that great smile of hers and a kiss. Yes, on the cheek but, meaningfully. "You look like you've been at it all day."

I nod.

"First order of business. I've decided you need a glass of wine. Sit down in the living room. I've started a fire. Check and see if it's okay."

I do as ordered. I give the fire the required stirring and collapse onto the couch. I hadn't realized, until Kristen mentioned it, how much has gone down today. My internal engine is operating on fumes. I wonder if a glass of wine will put me to sleep.

Kristen enters the room without making a sound. Or did I nod off? Nevertheless, I'm aware of her presence. Maybe it's a hint of her perfume. She hands me a glass of wine and curls up on the floor between me and the fire.

"Cheers!" she offers.

I'm too tired to think of a reply. I simply raise my glass and take a sip.

"Stephen, are you okay? I guess that's a stupid question. You've been with Deputy Director Mays for at least part of the day and..."

I'm torn. She wants to know what's going on. No fault there. But is there another reason? That's the dilemma. Who can I trust? I sound like a broken record. I don't think the current generation even understands what that means. "Give me a moment to reflect and enjoy the wine, the fire, and your company," I reply.

She raises her glass. "If I can help by listening, fine. If I can help by talking, fine. If I can help by shutting up altogether, that's fine also."

This woman is something else. I make an executive decision, which I hope to hell is the right one. I am going to trust Kristen. Notwithstanding what everyone else says, I am going to tell her everything. I'm already withholding information from the FBI and, after the notes on my windshield, from probably whomever it is that Galjarian works for as well.

161

Dammit, I hope I'm not being influenced by my feelings for her. And how is it that within two days, this lady's got me wrapped around her little finger? On one hand I sense that she is being completely herself but on the other hand there are too many questions and too few answers. I've simply got to talk to someone other than myself. I take a deep breath. "Let's just enjoy the moment."

She nods, turns, and prods the fire again.

Less than a minute passes, which seems like a wonderful eternity. Kristen uncoils herself from the floor, rises, and goes to the cabinet, which houses an entertainment center. Suddenly, Vivaldi floods the room. She approaches me, lifts my chin, and kisses me...on the lips this time.

"Everything will be all right," she gently whispers. "It's got to be."

She turns and walks into the kitchen. A few moments later, she returns with the bottle of wine, fills my glass, and tops off hers as well.

The last thing I want to do is talk about death and disease.

Sensing my mood, which she seems to do so well, she slips next to me on the couch and places her head on my shoulder.

I haven't felt this calm in a long time, and considering what's going on in the real world, the effect this woman is having on me is nothing less than miraculous. I start to calculate how much time I have before I need to prepare for tomorrow's meeting with the boys at ten and my noon tête-à-tête with the mystery man or woman.

"Maybe I'll just throw something simple together and we can stay in," Kristen whispers. "You look like you couldn't move anyway."

I merely blink in agreement, expending whatever energy I have left. Kristen gently glides away toward the kitchen.

I fall asleep.

I have no idea whether an hour, a day, or a week has passed, but the smell of garlic awakens me from repose. Vivaldi is still playing, and Kristen is in the kitchen making something that smells heavenly. I am reminded of the great line from the movie *Field of Dreams*, when one of the ball players asks Kevin Costner, "Is this heaven?" and he answers, "No, it's Iowa."

I suddenly feel uncomfortable. I look down and notice that I've spilled about two-thirds of a glass of wine onto my lap when I dozed off. At least I didn't break the glass. Now

what? My crotch is soaked and I feel really stupid. As I lift myself up from the couch, Kristen walks in and immediately starts to laugh. I am just a bundle of fun, I guess.

"I'm sorry," she giggles, "but I did that to myself last week when I was so tired I fell asleep with a wine glass in my hand. You're lucky. I spilled a glass of Merlot all over beige pants. White wine won't stain."

I smile. She can make me feel good even after I make a complete ass of myself.

"I've got an idea." She is smiling. "Take a shower and I'll put your pants in the dryer. Then you'll be refreshed and dry." She smiled.

"I've got a change of clothes in the car, and a shower will clear out the cobwebs."

"Great."

I retreat to the trunk of the Volvo, retrieve my tennis bag, open the shirt box, snag a clean shirt, and return. Kristen reaches out, gently grabs my hand, and leads me upstairs to a fabulous bathroom.

"Give me your pants." There is a sparkle in her eye, as she snaps her fingers.

"With pleasure." I try to be modest and flirtatious at the same time.

"You've got fifteen minutes, and then I'll turn off the hot water."

I empty my pockets on the double-sink counter, remove my belt with as much flair as I can muster, and place my pants in her outstretched hand. I am now standing in my boxers in front of a woman who has stolen my heart, or maybe my mind, and feeling not the least bit uncomfortable.

"Towels are on the shelf behind you. Shampoo and conditioner are in the shower."

"When does the fifteen minutes start?"

She exaggerates a look at her watch. "Four…three…two…one…liftoff ."

The door closes, and I am left alone in two rooms that are bigger than many people's living rooms. The room in which I'm standing houses a large double-sink vanity with an eight-foot mirror and built-in shelves and closet. A half wall separates the sinks from a toilet. Everything is marble and tile. But wait, through a door at the far end of the sink room is the shower room. Well, shower and tub room, featuring a Jacuzzi and a shower with two heads, each individually controlled. Fifteen minutes won't be enough time, especially if I spend it gawking at the fixtures. I turn on a showerhead and set the temperature on warm. I need to gauge the heat before I ease the water down to cool, or maybe I should make it cold. What am I saying? I'm getting way ahead of myself.

Shower therapy really is an art form when you can adjust not only the temperature, but the water pressure, with two different shower heads. I begin to realize that my fifteen-minute limit was imposed as a matter of water conservation.

I locate a bath sheet and begin to dry myself off, when I hear a discreet knock on the door. I wrap the towel around myself and cross the sink room to the door. Kristen hands me my pants, not only dried but pressed. Then she breaks out in laughter. Geez, my body isn't that bad.

Barely able to catch her breath, she says, "Stephen, you look like a lobster." Her laughter is bringing tears to her eyes.

Slowly, I swivel to face the mirror. Bright red is certainly an apt description of my skin. Boiled to perfection by the shower.

Trying to keep a straight face, I say, "You may dip me in butter if you wish."

Now she turns bright red, beginning with her neck and spreading over her full face. I have accomplished the impossible. I have successfully embarrassed the unflappable Ms. Marks.

"Red strawberries are best dipped in chocolate, but that's for dessert. Get dressed!" She gives her head a little shake, retreats out the door, then waves as she returns downstairs to attend to whatever she's been preparing.

After shaving and showering, I start to head downstairs, but my curiosity turns me down the hall to a closed door. Three bedroom doors are open, so why is this one, set on the short wall at the end of the hall, closed? I slip off my loafers and silently tiptoe across the hardwood floor without arousing Kristen's suspicions. My hand turns the knob and I slowly push open the door. It barely clears the first of multiple piles of boxes and files stacked four to five tiers high. I can't even see the floor! Manila files with sheets of paper poking out of all sides are sandwiched between the boxes, which keep them from spilling their contents onto the floor. The windows on both walls are blocked except for the casements along the tops. Then there's the smell — like a giant vacuum cleaner whose bag hasn't been changed in years. Not musty, but dusty. I close the door, slink back to the bathroom, slip on my loafers, and walk to the staircase. So much for a filing system.

I enter the living room, which Kristen has transformed into a dining area. A low table, properly adorned with linen and silver, faces the now-roaring fire. Maybe this is heaven. It's certainly not Iowa.

Kristen enters with two plates heaped high with pasta dressed with garlic, garden-fresh basil, sun-dried tomatoes, and chicken. She produces a bottle of Ruffino Chianti and says, "Try not to spill this on your pants. It not only stains, it would also be a terrible waste of a very good wine." She pours each of us a glass and snuggles in beside me. *"Buon appetito."*

We eat in silence, save the crackling of the fire and the haunting tones of Yo-Yo Ma's cello. The pasta is delectable, the wine ideal, the ambience perfect.

Why do I feel like shit?

Could it be that I want to unburden everything that happened during the course of the day, or do I want to forget everything and wrap Kristen in my arms and never let go? If I truly confide in her, maybe together we can make some sense of what is going on. Then we will have plenty of time for arm wrapping.

Maybe I should just seize the moment. Would that be irresponsible and selfish? This problem isn't of my making. It's been thrown at me like a ton of manure, which is beginning to stink.

"I feel very comfortable with you, and I'm happy you're here," Kristen says. "But I can't help but notice that you're really tense, and I hope I'm not the cause."

"No, you're the cure. It's just that I can't compartmentalize well enough to forget everything that's happened in the past couple of days."

"If it would make you feel better, you can tell me what's going on, and I'll try and help you work through whatever it is."

Damn, she looks good in the firelight. "Everything is so upside-down. A week ago I was alone, trying to sort out my life, hoping for something I could sink my teeth into. Now here I am, strongly attracted to you, dealing with a life-and-death crisis, and up to my neck in something that has more twists and turns than Storrow Drive."

"Stephen, last week I was alone, trying to sort out my life, and into my third temporary job of the year. Now, I'm also strongly attracted to you, trying to come to grips with the potential enormity of this thing, and way over my head."

Our lips touch. Not in the desperate, clutching sort of way you see in movies, but tenderly. As dumb as it sounds, I feel a tingle throughout my whole body. Should I pull her close to me? What should I do with my hands? As always, she answers the question by taking my hand and placing it on her cheek. It seems as though an hour passes before we part.

"That was nice," she murmurs. "As soon as we have taken care of business, or at least as much as we can, let's run away somewhere."

Wonderful thought. She brings me back to reality without letting the passion of the moment dissipate. Wow.

I stand, collect the dishes, and take them into the kitchen. When I return, I find that Kristen has turned the lights up a little brighter. When I enter the room, she presents two pads of paper and pencils.

"Let's see what we can add to what we both know."

She has no idea what she's gotten herself into.

"I hope you're ready for this."

I feel a chill. Looking at the fireplace, I realize that it is down to glowing embers. "I can't believe it's almost midnight." I stare at my watch. At least Kristen now knows everything that I do. I still have an uneasy feeling that I don't know everything she knows, however. It's essential that I either overcome this nagging doubt or disengage, which would be hard to do after telling her state secrets.

With a look that could melt even the hardest of granite, she says, "You may find this hard to accept…"

Shit, here it comes.

"…but I really had no idea when Robert called me to take on the interim position that I was walking into a time bomb. I've tried to keep up a strong front at work, and especially with the investors, basically because I'm dependent upon them for a job, but I've cried myself to sleep the last four days since we discovered the Ebola was missing. This is something no amount of business school prepares you for. I'm scared and not ashamed to admit it, and now you're dragged in. The only good thing about this mess is that I've met you." She gives me her incredible smile.

Over the last ten years I have learned, the hard way of course, that if something seems too good to be true, it usually is. But Kristen seems to change all that, unless she's the world's best actress. She certainly says everything I want to hear.

Reality returns as the grandfather clock in the hall chimes twelve. "I've got to go," I almost shout in alarm, "or I'll turn into a pumpkin."

Kristen stands up and says, in a voice that reminds me of my mother, "You're going to stay here, in the guest room. You're too tired to drive home and be back here by seven."

"Seven?" I'm totally confused.

"You don't think I'm going to let you spend almost four hours of our evening going over everything that's happened and then let you walk into that meeting without a plan? But first we've got to sleep on it. Get a few hours of quality sleep and wake up bright-eyed and bushy-tailed."

This lady is amazing.

"You get a guest room, and don't think for a moment

you'll be able to sneak into my room. Three German shepherds are guarding the door. Although if you scratch them behind the ears, they'd probably let you in. Be that as it may, you need a good night's sleep and there will be plenty of time after this is over."

She halts her own sentence in midstream. I think the bravado she's been displaying is beginning to slide.

I get up and pull her into my arms and begin to lead her upstairs, to which room I'm not certain, and to do what, even less certain. The fire is now virtually extinguished, and the screen will protect the rug from any random sparks. Kristen nestles her head in my shoulder. She points to her room at the top of the stairs, facing the street, which also faces south, the best light. Not a dog in sight. I put her down on the bed, pull the covers around her, and give her a quick kiss. I turn off the light, return to the landing, and begin my search for a guest room.

There are three to choose from. Any bed looks good. I slide out of my clothes, except boxer shorts, in case there's a fire or something in the middle of the night and I'd have to get up in a hurry. You know what I mean. I lie down and watch my own eyes close.

I fall asleep immediately.

I have a vague sense of hearing the clock strike three, when my door opens noiselessly. Although a Lanz night-gown covers her from head to toe, I immediately recognize Kristen, padding across the room towards me. I pretend to be asleep. To my surprise and delight, she crawls under the covers and snuggles next to me. Her movements suggest nothing sexual, simply the desire to be close, to give and receive comfort. I adjust my position and put my arm around her. She kisses me lightly, smiles, and falls fast asleep.

So do I.

CHAPTER TWENTY-FOUR

I am not ashamed to admit that waking up with a beautiful woman in my arms is an excellent way to start the day, even if that woman is draped in four yards of flannel. I slide out of bed and stare at the sleeping Kristen, and I find it hard to accept that she might have another agenda. I silently gather my clothes and head for the shower. Hot or cold?

After discovering that my former tennis, now overnight bag is well enough supplied to allow a change of clothes, a shave with a moderately sharp razor, and a few other personal things, I'm ready to face the day. What I'm going to do is still very much up in the air, but at least I'm reasonably rested, clean, and strangely at ease. I return to the bedroom to check up on Kristen, but she has retreated to her own room. I hope she's not upset. Nothing happened. Really! I decide to put a pot on the stove to boil some water for that ever-essential first cup of tea. As I descend the stairs, I hear what might pass for singing, were it not off key.

Kristen is bustling around the kitchen. The water is already on the stove, and what looks like an omelet with onions, peppers, cheese, and spicy Italian sausage is simmering. Kristen winks at me, and without skipping a beat, slices two English muffins, which she slides into the toaster oven. "Good morning, sunshine."

My knees nearly buckle.

"And thank you for giving me the first good night's sleep I've had in weeks." She brings my face close to hers, kisses me, and returns to her culinary chores. "I think you should call Ed's office and postpone your ten o'clock meeting. We need the time to think about what's happening, and prepare for your noon rendezvous. If you call now, you can leave a voice message for him, since no one will be in the office this early, and you're not home, so he won't be able to reach you except by cell, which you can turn off ."

I glance at my watch. It's about twenty minutes to eight, and she's right that no self-respecting VC will be in the office at this ungodly hour. I grab my i-phone and dial. I'm already half-wrong. The phone rings once, and the voice of one of the twin receptionists answers, "Good morning, Capital Investments, how may I direct your call?"

"Mr. Harris, please."

"Whom shall I say is calling?" Shit, that means he's already there.

"Stephen Blackman." I respond, still hoping to get into Ed's voicemail.

"Mr. Blackman, Mr. Harris is in a meeting with Mr. Barnett and another gentleman. Would you like me to interrupt him?"

"No, voicemail is fine." I breathe a sigh of relief. I wonder who the *other gentleman* is.

"Hi, this is Ed Harris. I can't come to the phone right now, but if you would leave a message and a number, I'll get back to you as soon as possible. Speak after the tone."

"Ed, Steve. Something has come up, and I can't make our ten o'clock meeting. How about later in the afternoon? I'll call you around one to confirm. Bye." I hang up.

"Well, that's done." I turn toward Kristen, who is now deftly lifting the omelet onto a plate.

"English muffins okay?"

"Yes'm." I do my best John Wayne imitation. "Mighty kind of you inviting a stranger in for some grub."

"Stranger, no. Strange, yes." She smiles. "Eat up, partner, we've got a lot to do. I'm going upstairs to make myself presentable. Your tea is steeping on the stove." She walks deliberately toward me, kisses me once again, and says, "You are quite special."

She retires upstairs, leaving me alone to eat a wonderful breakfast. At the end of the table rests today's *Boston Globe*, *The Wall Street Journal*, and *New York Times*. Decisions, decisions. I reach for the *Globe's* sports section. So much for being an intellectual.

I don't hear Kristen reenter the kitchen. I'm standing at the sink rinsing my dishes, as I was trained to do by my mother from a tender age.

"I'll put some more water on and grab a couple of pads and pencils, and we'll try to sort out fact from fiction." Kristen is all business, except for the jeans and sweater she's wearing.

We try to create a matrix of facts and put the various players into the appropriate positions. Nothing really works, especially the tension between Mays and Galjarian. And then there's Jacob Kettleman, the wild card. I look at my watch again and notice that it's almost ten. I hope I haven't created havoc with Ed, who is already edgy, and Galjarian, who is — I'm really not sure. I resist the temptation to check my cell phone for messages, deciding that the less I know about who is trying to reach me, the better off I'll be.

What we know already is a lot less important than what we don't know. Consider the following: Three men disappear; one is found with a bullet in his head in his own garage. I need to remind myself to ask what the coroner set as a time of death. All evidence of their research is systematically cleaned out of GSS and their house looks like it was hit by a Kansas tornado. *We're off the see the wizard...*

"Kristen, what if Onellon, Gordon, and Kettleman were worried about someone stealing or sabotaging their work, and they preemptively took off and went into hiding? They realized that they needed to get something from the house, Gordon went back to get whatever it was, and in the process interrupted whoever was tossing the place and got killed. Let's presume that the people from whom they were fleeing were the same people who were turning the house upside down, looking for a clue as to where the three had gone."

"Okay, but that doesn't explain the tension between the FBI and, I guess, the Department of Defense." Kristen is still in shock about the new role Robert Galjarian has assumed in this whole thing.

"If we presume that the tension that exists between those agencies has its roots in any one of a number of things unrelated to this situation, we're being diverted." I lean on the kitchen counter.

"Is terrorism at the core of the problem, or could it be money? If the research is as good as I've been led to believe, we're talking billions. And people have killed for a lot less."

"I'm getting nervous about my noon meeting. It could mean nothing or everything. We've got to make a plan."

Kristen's eyes narrow slightly. "Without sounding too dramatic, do you think you should go to Fanueil Hall alone?"

"There will be tens of thousands of people at lunchtime."

"Have you looked outside?"

I hadn't yet, but I do so now. Yesterday's bright November day has literally been washed away by a steady, cold rain that's still falling. Kristen is right. There aren't going to be many people strolling among the carts and outdoor cafés in forty-degree rain.

"Now what?"

"Let's make a plan."

CHAPTER TWENTY-FIVE

We leave Cambridge a little after eleven. I'm not worried about traffic or even parking. I am, however, worried about Kristen. What if this turns out to be dangerous? And furthermore, I was specifically told to come alone. With only a few stragglers loitering around the market area, Kristen will be conspicuous and maybe screw things up. Maybe even get hurt. There is no way I'm going to convince her to stay at home, or even in the car. She announces that she will go to a coffee shop at the far end of Quincy Market, about one hundred yards from Fanueil Hall, and wait for thirty minutes. If I don't come and meet her, she will call Galjarian and Mays, in that order, and tell them everything. At least someone cares.

We decide to park in the garage near City Hall and walk from there. I wonder if we're being watched. The chill down my spine matches the weather outside. I leave the car first and tell Kristen to wait five minutes, then take a different route.

Walking down Union Street, just past the Holocaust Memorial, I am drawn into the parallel between that era and our own. Call it ethnic cleansing, genocide or just plain murder, it's all the same.

This is going to be a day I'll never forget, or is it?

I cross over into the Fanueil Hall/Quincy Market complex, past the statue of Sam Adams, the man, not the beer. I look nervously at my watch. It's only 11:54. I slowly continue toward the open area designated as my meeting place. There are fewer than a dozen people milling about. On a nice summer day, there can be as many as a thousand people in this space. I start to consider those around me more closely. What exactly am I looking for? My guess is either Lazlo Onellon or Jacob Kettleman. The place suddenly livens up when a busload of fourth- or fifth-graders disembark from a school bus. As I watch the kids stretch their legs, I am jostled by a smallish man, wearing a trench coat. He looks a lot like Danny DeVito.

"Here, read this." He pushes a piece of paper in my hand, turns, and walks away.

"Wait!" I shout.

But he keeps walking, more quickly than before. I debate running after him, but then what? Grab him and beat the shit out of him until he tells me what's going on? I don't think so.

I open the plain white envelope. "Oh my God!"

Mr. Blackman.
   Thank you for keeping our appointment. I am sure you appreciate the need for caution. Would you and Ms. Marks join us in thirty minutes at Old

North Church? I suggest you walk, since parking in the North End is often very difficult. You can pick up Ms. Marks on the way. I understand her presence and do not consider it a breach of faith.

The letter is unsigned. My heart rate picks up to about two hundred beats per minute. I feel flushed and about ready to pass out.

"Stephen, are you all right?"

I spin around. "Kristen! What are you doing here?"

"A funny little man, who looks like Danny DeVito just walked right up to me and said I should meet you here. What's happening?"

I hand her the letter.

Her eyes dart back and forth. She looks at me with an almost pleading expression. "What's going on?"

"We are going to take a scenic stroll back to Boston's Historic North End and visit the church made famous by Paul Revere. Other than that, I haven't got the foggiest." I attempt to sound brave, but inside I'm trembling.

She laces her arm through mine. "Whoever it is, we've been watched for some time now, haven't we?"

"Remember, these guys are running, probably for their lives, and Kettleman is a trained intelligence officer. They don't know either of us from Adam. I'd be damned careful, too. I'm sure that from the moment I left the parking garage yesterday, and maybe even before, I've been followed. He knew you were with me, where you were sitting, and had the ability to respond within seconds." I turn and pull her toward me. "Everything will be okay."

"Promise?"

"Boy Scout's honor."

We once again start toward the Old North Church. *One if by land, two if by sea.* It takes only about five minutes, despite the construction obstacles, to reach the church. Now what? Go inside. An organ recital is in progress, and we slide into a back pew. Bach. Haunting and beautiful. Kind of like Ms. Marks.

I virtually jump out of my skin when I feel a hand on my shoulder. It's the little man in the trench coat. He hands me another note.

> *Stay for the concert. Leave by the side entrance and walk to 345 Hanover Street and ring the middle buzzer twice. You will be let in.*
> *Thank you for your patience.*

I assume the invitation still applies to Kristen as well. By the time I've read the message, the deliverer has already disappeared. I pass the note to Kristen. A look crosses her face that I can't quite describe. Is she perplexed or scared or both? If she's feeling anything like I am, both.

I put my hand over hers. She clutches it a little too tightly. We listen to the balance of the concert, which I think is good, but truth be known, my heart isn't in it. We slip out the side door as instructed and zigzag our way to Hanover Street, the North End's main drag. Under normal circumstances, I would love a stroll through the alleyways of Boston's increasingly yuppified Little Italy, especially with Kristen. But there's a sense of urgency in the notes, so I decide that time is of the essence.

Wedged between a bakery, which I will visit when we're through with whatever awaits us, and a drugstore, the old-fashioned kind, is number 345.

I ring the bell twice. My heart once again thumps over a hundred beats per minute. The door opens, and unless he has a twin, Jacob Kettleman, looking a little the worse for wear, is extending his hand, beckoning us to enter.

As we cross the threshold, he immediately closes the door behind us.

"I'm sorry for all the cloak-and-dagger, but it was absolutely essential." Kettleman speaks with just a touch of a British accent. "Please, come on up. It will be quite a bit more comfortable, and it's very secure."

We ascend a flight of well-traveled stairs and enter an apartment that is so incongruous with the neighborhood I almost break out in laughter. The entire place is so high-tech — modern and really well done. Partially open to the second floor and connected by a wooden spiral staircase is yet another floor. The entire place screams white, wood, leather, and electronics.

"We've kept the downstairs as a rather plain apartment, while the basement is a state-of-the-art laboratory," Kettleman says. He seems indifferent, especially in light of the fact that one of his colleagues has had his head blown off , that state and federal agencies are searching for him, and potentially billions of dollars of research is not yet accounted for. Not to mention the Ebola.

He swivels toward a monitor on the wall and speaks into it. "Our guests have arrived."

Cameras move back and forth throughout the apartment.

"We'll be right up," an invisible male voice responds. "There's iced tea in the fridge, and a tray of sushi."

"Please make yourselves comfortable. You can freshen

up over there." Kettleman gestures toward a partially open door.

Kristen looks at me. Her mouth is still hanging open. "Thank you," she says, and wanders off toward the indicated bathroom.

"Mr. Blackman, or may I call you Stephen? I promise you that within less than an hour's time, everything will be made clear."

"Stephen is fine." I am taken far aback. How did Alice feel when she fell down the rabbit hole?

"Please call me Jacob," he says, crossing toward the kitchen, which looks like Williams-Sonoma meets *Gourmet* or Microsoft meets *Architectural Digest*. Opening the largest Sub-Zero refrigerator I have ever seen, he removes a pitcher of what appears to be the aforementioned iced tea, along with a large serving platter. Our host places five glasses on the counter, fills a silver bucket with ice cubes from the ice machine, cuts up a lemon, and fills the five glasses. Five? Time for a head count — Kristen, Jacob Kettleman, presumably Onellon, and me. That's four. And probably the Danny DeVito look-alike?

I'm losing it. Thank God Kristen is returning. I need to splash some cold water on my face. I pass back through the living room toward the bathroom, followed the whole way by the surveillance cameras.

The entire apartment blends form and function to perfection. Each piece of furniture integrates seamlessly into the room, and announces itself unmistakably as custom-made. If these guys designed this place themselves, they could quit their day job. What am I talking about? They did quit their day job.

Kristen whispers, "This place is incredible."

I nod. Not only is each furnishing remarkable, even the floors combine stone, wood, and marble, each material complementing the other. Of course, high-quality antique Oriental rugs adorn the bare spots. I am baffled, to say the least.

By the time I wash up and open the bathroom door, I hear voices. I quickly stride into the living area and almost fall over. Three men are standing next to Kristen, each holding a glass of iced tea: Jacob Kettleman, Lazlo Onellon, and Theodore Gordon. I am tempted to head back into the bathroom — whether to splash more water on my face or throw up, I'm not sure. Sensing my unsteadiness, Onellon rushes over and grabs my elbow.

"Please sit down. I promised you that I would explain everything, and I will," Jacob Kettleman announces.

I'm numb, but I do as I'm told. Both Onellon and Gordon extend their hands to me.

"Hi, I'm Ted, Ted Gordon."

I nod and automatically shake his hand.

"And I'm Lazlo Onellon," the second man says. "We're pleased to meet you, and apologize for the mess you've been drawn into. We're grateful that you're here."

I meekly look over at Kristen. She rolls her eyes and shrugs her shoulders. Great help.

"It's past lunch, and I know you haven't had anything to eat. Ted made some sushi, and I guarantee it is fabulous."

Ted blushes.

"Whoa!" I say to myself. This whole thing is off the charts.

Kristen and I are offered a variety of little rice rolls with things in the middle, mostly raw fish. A drizzle of green wasabi and sliver-thin slices of fresh ginger adorn the side of the platter. I know from painful past experience that wasabi can dissolve taste buds at thirty feet.

"Shrimp, salmon, tuna, and squid." Gordon points to the tray.

"Three yeses…and one no."

"These are delicious," Kristen says.

I nod in agreement, but say nothing. My mouth is full. Surprise. Since the tray has been placed within arm's reach, I decide to take another — and another. I hadn't realized how hungry I am. The problem is that sushi is tasty but not filling. I fondly remember the bakery downstairs — later.

Jacob settles himself into a large leather and stainless chair that appears to be suspended in thin air. The base of the chair is formed by transparent micro-thin fibers. Cool design.

"I think I had better start at the beginning," he remarks.

Good place to begin — the beginning.

CHAPTER TWENTY-SIX

"We three met at a conference in Israel a few years ago," Jacob begins, his voice exuding a quiet assurance. "I had just received my MBA from MIT and had returned to Israel to explore employment opportunities.

"I had completed undergraduate studies in engineering and physics at the Tel Aviv University and continued my studies at Cambridge University. I fulfilled my mandatory military duty in the Israeli army in intelligence."

He's being refreshingly candid.

"When I met Lazlo and Ted, we hit it off immediately. We liked the same kind of things, from music to art to food. We talked for hours, and I decided that I would return to the United States and try to organize a company around their research, and raise the necessary capital. What they were doing was important, and being involved from almost the beginning was an exciting opportunity. We seemed to energize one another."

He pauses.

"Despite what you may have heard from any one of a number of sources, I don't work for any government agency — Israeli or American. The intelligence community is rather tight-knit, and you often meet people who are doing the same things you are. You develop friendships based on kindred spirit. You are doing something that you can't discuss with anyone on the outside, therefore you spend an ever-increasing amount of time on the inside. The result is a little group of self-absorbed people with no lives outside their own world. Traditional enemies are now allies, and the current enemy is basically faceless." Kettleman sounds angry.

"If you leave the inner circle, you seldom see any of your prior contacts, unless, of course, they remain in intelligence, which somehow gives them a license to call upon you for whatever scraps of information they're trying to get. The longer you're out of the loop, the less frequently you get calls, largely because your information becomes stale. It never totally stops, and those who are still on the inside can't get it through their heads that not everyone wants to remain a member of their club."

This guy seems like the real McCoy. And it certainly explains the Galjarian/Mays tension.

"More sushi or iced tea?" Ted pipes in.

"Yes, please," Kristen and I simultaneously respond.

"Kind of like once a spook, always a spook?" I say.

"Simply put, but accurate, unless you want out, in which event it is assumed that you're only taking on the guise of an outsider because you've got the soul of an insider. It's scary how intense these people are. And they're the good guys. I don't want to get started on the psychological makeup of the bad guys. It's beyond comprehension. But back to the story."

I'm impressed with Jacob Kettleman.

"Although I promised you that I would make everything clear in an hour, it may take more time than that. Are there any calls you need to make? We have a secure line."

He must have read my mind. What am I going to do about Ed and Robert, who are probably wearing out the carpet at Capital Investments, pacing back and forth wondering where the hell I've gone? This seems like a far better use of my time. If Jacob's description of the intelligence community is correct, and I have every reason to believe it is, and if he truly feels the way his words, tone, and body language indicate and provided I'm not being conned, then the further I stay away from both Mays and Galjarian and the closer I stay to the North End trio, the better my chances are to put this mess behind me.

"Other than to take a quick pit stop from time to time, I'm here for the duration," I announce.

Kristen gives me a quick look. She must know that I'm thinking about the meeting.

"I'd like another piece of sushi," she chimes in. Rising and walking toward the kitchen, she places her arm around the surprised Ted Gordon.

It's magic. She picked up all my signals, processed them, and came to the same conclusion as I, all without exchanging a word. I get up and make my way to the bathroom once more.

"Would you like something else to drink?" Lazlo Onellon asks me on my return.

"I love the iced tea, but it simply flows through me."

He smiles in acknowledgment and retreats to the kitchen. I notice that Jacob Kettleman is gone. Like vanished. Then I see him descending from the third floor.

"Only one bathroom downstairs, and as much as I like the iced tea, it flows right through me." He walks across the room.

There is definitely something I like about this guy.

As I take my glass from Lazlo's hand, I notice a flashing red light next to the communication box.

Lazlo and Jacob exchange glances and together they approach the panel. Each enters a code. The panel buzzes the downstairs door open.

Jacob turns to me. "Can't be too careful. We each have a personal code that changes every twelve hours, and two codes are required to open the door."

As he speaks, Lazlo walks to the head of the stairs and looks at the monitor that scans the front foyer and stairs. He nods, and Jacob pushes the keypad once again. Lazlo opens the door, and in walks one of the most attractive women I have ever seen. I hope Kristen doesn't see my jaw drop. She and Lazlo immediately embrace. I confess, I'm jealous and confused as hell.

"Stephen, Kristen, I would like you to meet my wife, Sarah."

I resist running across the room to shake her hand. I simply follow Kristen. Sarah Onellon is equal in stature to Lazlo's six-foot-plus height, with long red hair, light brown eyes, and legs that don't stop. Her handshake is firm. She purposefully walks over to Jacob and gives him a kiss, warm, but not as intense as the one which she gave her husband. She then turns to Ted Gordon, who, like a puppy dog that doesn't want to be left out, has moved beside the towering woman. She gives him a hug and a kiss on the cheek. The psychodynamics of this group are complicated, made more so when Jacob announces, "Sarah is my sister."

Before I can recover any cognitive powers, Sarah adds, "I'm glad to meet both of you. Hopefully, with your help, this rather unpleasant affair can end." Her foreign accent is faint.

"Sarah," Lazlo says, "we're in the middle of explaining the situation. You're welcome to join us."

"I'll join you for a little while, if only to try and keep some gender balance." She smiles, as does her brother.

"By way of explanation, Sarah is not only my sister, but holds a Ph.D. in oceanography and marine biology from USC," Jacob says. "She challenges Lazlo and Ted to seek answers outside traditional research. She's also our den mother and best friend."

Sarah turns her face away ever so slightly, then responds, "watching out for these three has become a full-time job."

"I think we need to return to the overview," Jacob states, "otherwise our guests will be here for the next two days."

"Should I make dinner arrangements?" Ted chimes in.

All eyes return to Kristen and me.

I take the initiative to answer. "I'm scheduled to meet with Ed Harris, Robert Galjarian, and probably Henry Barnett today." I've just taken a huge chance, bringing them into my confidence, but I don't seem to have any other choice. I'm afraid to look at Kristen.

Jacob interrupts. "Before you go on, you don't know us yet, and I think we can convince you that there's more to this incident than you know or even suspect. Sorting out good from bad is not that clear. Some of the good guys have been splattered with bad-guy paint and vice-versa. What we need is closure, and to extract the rotten tooth. The rest will then come together. None of the three men with whom you were to meet today are truly bad guys, although Bob — Robert fits into the category of fanatic. He's fabricated a life from bits and pieces of everything and everyone imaginable. He believes that the end justifies the means, but he's basically been on the right side of things. He's one of those who can't understand that there is a life beyond what he is doing. James

Bond would have been his best friend. Ed and Henry are simple investors, for whom this entire situation has grown beyond all their life experiences. They initially treated our disappearance as an in-house matter, and brought Kristen in for damage assessment. After they were confronted with the possibility that the Ebola might be missing, they had no choice but to bring in an outsider, but a discreet outsider. I'm not criticizing them, but they couldn't figure out what was going on and, therefore, couldn't be trusted by us. I don't want you to think that we took their investment money, completed research, and intended to run off and sell it at a higher price. It was the combination of Galjarian and the FBI that unnerved us. And there was no way Ed and Henry could be of any help."

"We've been briefed about everything in some detail," I offer. "So I think both Kristen and I are aware of the stakes. May I ask you some questions?"

He inclines his head. So do Lazlo, Sarah, and Ted.

"Up until two hours ago, I'd assumed that Ted had been murdered. I saw his body, or what was left of it. And now he's serving us sushi and tea. Let's start with that."

"Let me fill in some gaps in the story you've been told." Jacob Kettleman's voice has lowered an octave. He appears angry, blended with a sense of urgency. "We weren't kidnapped, nor is anything missing. We simply moved the research aspects of GSS because there was a breach of security. We've been planning the move for over six months, after it had become clear that the research could be compromised. We worked around the clock, with Sarah spearheading the operation to set up this secret facility. And in case you're wondering, Sarah was also an officer in Israeli intelligence. She and Lazlo have been married for almost a year."

"It'll be a year in ten days," Lazlo says with pride.

Kristen subtly slips her hand next to mine.

"We started to make duplicates of everything, and moved them away from GSS and from our rented house, which we began to use as a prop to divert attention away from here," Jacob says. "Everything in the Concord house was contrived. The computers contained useless information. We left nothing to chance. When we were ready, the only thing we had to relocate was the physical research. We took everything out of GSS over the long Columbus Day weekend and disappeared."

"For the last several days," I interrupt, "I have been motivated as much by fear as anything else, considering the likelihood that the world might be facing biological terrorism, and I was basically powerless to do anything about it. All along, you had everything safe under lock and key, several keys. Didn't you realize the panic you could have caused?"

"Jacob, let me speak for a moment." Sarah stands and directs her gaze toward me. "Stephen, Kristen, we were confident that the fact that the Ebola was missing would go unverified and unreported by GSS for at least as long as we needed to resolve the breach. Ebola research, as with any infectious disease, requires CDC approval, which, by the way, we have. However, we did violate a protocol by moving the Ebola to this location. Ted has been in contact with several key persons in Atlanta, and it's not a problem, given the state-of-the-art facility that we have.

"The problem arose when we sent an internal, confidential e-mail from Ted to Jacob, saying that GSS did not have permission for infectious disease research, and violation of the requirement meant fines and possibly imprisonment for corporate officers as well as directors. The memo was a fake, but it achieved the result we were seeking. Ed Harris called us up in a complete panic, saying that Bob Galjarian had told him he could be personally liable for unauthorized research and that we should get the necessary paperwork immediately.

"We knew we had a leak, and it looked like Bob was the source. The memo was not encrypted, but in plain text so that hacking it was not too difficult. It was the fact that someone was reading our mail that convinced us that we needed to implement our plan. It also meant that Ed wasn't going to blow the whistle on the missing Ebola until the last possible second."

I again glance over at Kristen, who looks troubled. "If everything is safe and sound here in the North End, why was Ted's death faked, and by whom?" I seem to be the only one troubled by the look-alike corpse.

"That wasn't predicted, nor was it connected to us in any way. The body, whoever it was, was placed there as a diversion. We are aware that our house has been visited on more than one occasion, and was ripped apart from top to bottom. You were intended to presume that someone was looking for something in the house, and that Ted accidentally interrupted them and was killed as a result."

I shrug.

"We were very careful and thorough." Jacob speaks with pride, not arrogance. "Surveillance cameras were installed around the property. Everything is on tape."

A bead of perspiration has formed on Kristen's lip. I'm not sure whether it's the relief of finding the Ebola and the missing research, or Jacob's comments about the murderer being on tape. Something was touching a nerve.

"Jacob, isn't it simply a matter of going to the authorities with your material and getting the bad guys arrested?"

"Yes and no. To whom do you suggest we go?"

"I think you know a lot more than I do about the players, so I'm not in a position to comment, except that there must be at least one person out there that you can trust."

"Just because you're paranoid, doesn't mean someone isn't out there following you." A smile appears on Jacob's lips. "It's been almost three hours."

I look at my watch. Yeah, I'm still hungry, but I'm also worried about Kristen. "What time does the bakery close downstairs?" Since the world isn't going to end tomorrow, at least I can get some fresh cannoli. All work and no food makes Stephen grumpy.

No sooner said than Ted opens the Sub-Zero and produces yet another platter, stacked with fresh Italian pastries. For a change, I am speechless. Turning toward Kristen, I notice that her usual smile is gone, and she looks as though she's seen a ghost. Now I'm getting *really* worried.

"Are you okay?" I know it's a dumb question, especially if something Jacob had said about the killer has upset her, but it's worth a try.

"I'm pissed, really pissed." Her voice is surprisingly harsh, and louder than I had anticipated. Everyone turns in unison. "I've been used by Galjarian, and was half-scared to death that the world could end tomorrow. I've had one night's sleep in the past week, and I'm God damned mad. Let's just get the bastard who's behind all this shit and string him up."

I don't know whether to applaud or hug her. I choose the latter, while the other members of the audience stand by in silent approval.

With a sense of theatrical timing surpassed only by Orson Welles, Ted Gordon says, "First some cannoli and maybe some Pinot Grigio...then let's get the bastard."

I definitely feel a lot better. Kristen puts her hands on my cheeks and gives me a kiss, a serious smooch.

I wolf down three cannoli, one of which is double chocolate, and absolutely decadent, together with two glasses of a nice wine. "I'm going to call Ed Harris."

"Do you think that would be wise? I suggest you

wait until after we've completed our discussion and viewed the surveillance tapes and taken a moment to reflect." Jacob makes the question sound like a statement of fact.

"I don't intend to engage him in any sort of dialogue, but rather to let him know that we're fine and on the job. If Robert Galjarian is who you say he is, I don't want him to start searching for us, finding my car in the parking garage, asking people at Quincy Market, maybe getting a tip that someone saw us in the North End, and bring him to your doorstep."

"Feel free to call. Your car is in Kristen's driveway, the shades are closed, music is playing, a fire has been burning all day, and an occasional burst of laughter can be heard. The mail was brought in and the paper will be as well. Several calls have been made to both Capital Investments and GSS from Kristen's home phone, leaving messages that you were in a meeting, a very important meeting, and would call later.

"Bravo!" I bow slightly.

Theoretically, my job is over. I found Lazlo Onellon, Ted Gordon, and Jacob Kettleman, plus another Kettleman-Onellon to boot. I found all the research, and I found the Ebola. I should quit while I'm ahead. Take the money and run. But who's responsible for necessitating the secret move in the first place, and how is he or she connected with the murder? Phase one is now complete. Phase two begins.

"Ted, may I have another cannoli?" I need to develop better self-control. I'm entitled. The world isn't going to end, and the fact that these are fresh cannoli and not cardboard donuts must be factored in. "Maybe just a half."

"I think we should view the surveillance tapes now." Jacob clears his throat. "The system we use is wireless, and each camera, eight altogether, sends images to a unit we have installed in the basement here, which records the images on a DVD. Some of the cameras operate when triggered by motion, while others are activated when a beam is interrupted. For example, when you drive up the driveway, a beam is broken. Same is true when you enter a door or window. The pictures are time coded, and when they're received, we put them in chronological order. It's somewhat like editing a motion picture, so what you'll be watching is sequential. Since the images are digital, I can stop and enlarge any frame."

I am duly impressed.

The room darkens, and a picture appears on what I had thought was an ordinary wall hanging. It's spooky. The image is indeed date and time coded. We begin on October 1 at 7:14 am. Ted can be seen as the garage door opens. He places a large stack of newspapers into a green bin. Recycling. He gets into the Range Rover and backs the car out into the driveway.

The angle switches, and we see Lazlo open the front door, stop and turn to whomever is inside, follow the gravel walk to the Range Rover, enter, and close the door. Seconds later, we see the Range Rover at the bottom of the driveway.

"I wanted to show you daylight footage before we get to the really interesting material, so you could become accustomed to the sequencing." Jacob leans forward.

I glance over at Kristen. Her eyes are glued to the screen.

"We're going to fast forward to October 5 now." Jacob starts the surveillance images once again.

The time is now 4:23 pm, and it is noticeably darker. An oil delivery truck enters the driveway and proceeds toward the house. The deliveryman removes the filler hose and drags it around the side. The camera angle changes once again, and we see him place some kind of device on each of several windows on the side and rear of the house. The driveway camera is reactivated. The deliveryman drags the hose back to the truck, winds it up, and leaves.

"Can we ask questions as we go along, or should we wait until the end?" I'm really getting into video. This is very neat stuff .

"Please interrupt at any time." Sarah smiles at me, then at her husband.

"Have you been able to identify the oil man, and what exactly are those devices he placed on the windows?"

"The oil man is Charles Flaherty. He lives in South Boston. No criminal record, works for a company called New England Home Heating Service. He's the brother-in-law of FBI Special Agent Fitzgerald."

I am shocked into silence.

Sarah never looks in my direction. "The listening devices Mr. Flaherty installed were wireless transmitters, much like our video cameras, but more primitive because they need to be attached to the window's glass. Since we did not want to expose the fact that we had found the devices, we simply put a piece of plastic wrap over the inside of the glass, so that the sound would be inaudibly garbled but not let on that the devices had been discovered." Very quickly, this is now becoming Sarah's show. "We are going to fast forward two days. The seventh. Ted and Lazlo have gone to a conference in New Haven, and Jacob is in the office." Sarah nods to her brother, who starts the tape once again.

At 10:34 am, a black Ford Crown Victoria with U.S. government plates drives up the driveway. The car stops in front of the garage, the passenger door opens, and out pops our friend Ken, the maintenance man, Agent Wells. I can't get a good look at the driver's face.

Ken walks up the path to the front door and enters the house, as cool as can be. He reappears about ten minutes later and shakes his head to the driver, whose features I still can't clearly see. What I've just viewed is impossible to reconcile with what the deputy director told me yesterday morning.

God damn it!

"Did you have any cameras inside?" I nervously tap my fingers on the arm of the chair.

"We didn't, because we felt that it would be substantially harder to hide the unit inside the house. If someone found an inside camera, then the perimeter units would be at risk, which we definitely did not want." Sarah has thought this out thoroughly.

"Have you been able to identify the driver or the plate?" Kristen has returned to the living room.

"No to the first, and more or less yes to the second. We've tried to enhance, enlarge, and do everything in the book to get a better image of the driver, but to no avail. The plates are registered to the FBI. The car is a standard motor pool vehicle, checked in and out each day. Except that this one was serviced on the seventh at a repair garage located in Charlestown and owned by William Harvey, who lives in South Boston, two doors down from Mr. Flaherty. The car was returned to the FBI pool at 4:30 pm, all tuned up and ready to go." Sarcasm drips from Sarah's words.

"I've seen enough to know that we can't trust the FBI. What should we do now?" Kristen's brow narrows.

"There are several more sequences that are extremely important," Jacob says.

Why is Kristen so anxious about these films?

"On Tuesday, the eighth, nothing worth mentioning happened," Sarah continues. "Ted stayed home most of the day to catch up on reading, Lazlo went to the office and then to Cambridge to meet me for a drink, and Jacob was in the office, making sure all the scientific data was backed up so that when we crashed the machines on Saturday, nothing would be permanently lost. On Wednesday, we had an interesting visit from *Media Cable*, which, before you ask, doesn't exist."

Once again the screen fills with a blue and white van,

the name *Media Cable* on the door. The van proceeds up the driveway and stops in front of the garage. The driver exits, walks toward the front door of the house, and appears to ring the doorbell. After less than a minute, he opens the door.

"The door was locked, so either he jimmied the door or had a key. We are of the belief that Ken made several copies and gave them out as needed."

Sarah is beginning to scare me. I feel my palms begin to sweat, and I never sweat. This is starting to look like an FBI-backed covert operation. No wonder everyone is paranoid.

Rather than watch an empty door for an hour, we fast forward again. The image reappears, with the TV man exiting the house, pretending to say good-bye to the occupant, getting in his van, and leaving. Fifty-seven minutes had passed, according to the time code.

"Prior to returning to the Concord house, we would always remotely access the video recording for the period we were gone." Ted sounds proud of their strategy.

Jacob replaces his sister as the narrator. "The video would tell us if security had been breached and give us the opportunity to debug any situation. Our visitor from the cable company placed a series of remote microphones throughout the house. He also did a reasonably careful job of going through files. He probably tried to make copies of the discs, but we disabled the CD writer. What he got is what we wanted him to get, anyway. Nothing but false trails.

"Ted was the first to see the tape because he was the first to return home. By cell, we scripted a phone call to me from the house, to be placed by Ted. We also had several frequency scramblers installed, so that our guests were unable to hear our conversations, except when we chose to let them listen. We don't know who the video man was. The plate on the van had been stolen several hours before the visit, and the van disappeared, although I suspect that the graphics were magnetic stick-ons and were removed when the van was ditched.

"Wednesday, Agent Wells visited us again, but this time, he has gone back into cover. He arrives, opens the garage, puts the trash barrels and recyclables in the back of his pickup truck, and leaves. He returns about forty minutes later with empty barrels. It appears as if he made a dump run, unless, of course, he took our trash to be screened, in which event, he was extremely disappointed. Thursday is really interesting."

The images again appear: two men wearing black from head to toe emerge from the woods behind the house. The timer indicates that it's about six in the morning and dawn is still an hour away.

"We're quite proud of this feature," Lazlo says as the screen suddenly brightens up, so that it appears to be high noon on a crystal-clear day. "Infrared enhancement, and not the store-bought variety. Right from a friend at MIT who is working on something for NASA. It's ironic that he won't tell me what it's for, but he will give me a demo."

The images move to within fifty feet of the house. One takes some kind of mini grappling hook from a bag he's carrying and throws it over a branch of a maple tree, behind which they have taken refuge.

"Good thing we hadn't used that tree ourselves." Ted starts to laugh.

The tape shows the two men installing a camera in the tree, aimed at the back of the house. If this were a Hollywood movie, they could call it *I Spy, You Spy*. I decide to keep my mouth shut, however.

"Needless to say, we weren't able to identify the two photographers, except to say that the equipment they installed was very sophisticated and expensive. No serial numbers, but I recognized the unit as being one which is available on the gray market for about $13,000, in cash. It has an Achilles' heel, however: even a small magnet placed within about two feet of the camera distorts its picture and renders it useless. We drilled several holes in the branches above, installed small refrigerator magnets, and covered the holes with sawdust and bark. It would take days to figure out what we had done. But at that point we didn't have days, and we knew it. Within forty-eight hours, we had disappeared." Jacob's eyes dart around the room. All faces are expressionless.

"Were you able to keep transmitting after you left?" I turn to Kristen, who shifts slightly in her seat.

Sarah again assumes control. "Definitely. And we've been able to maintain coverage undetected. The post-incident footage is even more interesting, especially the next couple of images."

"Nothing important happened until late Tuesday. Presumably it'd been discovered that we'd gone, along with the research," Jacob says.

The next segment is dated Tuesday, October 15, and is timed at 4:32 pm. A gray Mercedes sedan pulls up to the garage and out pops none other than Ed Harris. He strides up to the front door and appears to ring the doorbell — not once or twice, but constantly for about two minutes. He then opens his wallet and pulls out his business card, inserts it between the door and the jamb, and walks back to his car. His face bears a look of pure anger. Five minutes later, either by design or accident, Ken enters. He is less subtle. He unlocks the door to the house, enters, and stays about five minutes. He returns to his truck. We see him reach over and pick up a cell phone. After a short but animated call, he gets out of his truck and starts to walk around the house. Within a minute or two, a silver Ford Crown Victoria drives up. The plates are visible. It's the car Deputy Director Mays uses. Special Agent Fitzgerald opens the driver's door. We see Ken coming around the side. They both enter the house. Again, within a few minutes, they return to the driveway. They are screaming at each other, not in a hostile way, but rather like each of them has something more important to say than whatever the other is saying. Fitzgerald literally jumps into his car and smokes his tires down the driveway. So much for stealth. Ken follows, but at a more sedate pace. I wish there was sound.

"It's frustrating that we can't hear them, but the sound units are bigger and less reliable." Jacob anticipates my thought.

No shit.

"The next sequence is Thursday. I might add that Ken twice visited the house on Wednesday, but never left his truck."

The image is dated October 17, and the timer reads 10:21 am. Ken's truck enters the driveway, followed by Agent Fitzgerald. Ken enters the house and then emerges from the garage. He goes to the back of the truck and pulls a large rug-like object to the end of the tailgate. Fitzgerald grabs one end and Ken the other, and between them, they carry the parcel into the garage. The automatic door closes.

"That appears to answer the question of how the body got into the Range Rover, but not the question of who belongs to the body." This is getting uglier by the second.

"From what we've been able to ascertain, the corpse was a John Doe from the city morgue. Probably some poor homeless guy. He was selected because of his size and general features, and because he wouldn't be missed. He was most likely shot after being placed in the driver's seat."

Jacob is so matter-of-fact, it's unnerving. Somebody — let's be more accurate — two FBI agents, plant a dead body in Ted Gordon's car and then shoot it for effect. This is all too conspiratorial for me. I am drenched in perspiration. "I still don't understand the FBI's involvement."

"Let me finish with two or three more scenes and

then we can talk out some of these questions." Sarah seems eager to continue.

The next series of shots shows three men dressed in ninja-black suits entering the house from the woods. They stay for more than an hour and leave the same way. So much for how and when the house was tossed. The sequence from Saturday shows a VW convertible, owned by none other than Kristen, driving up the driveway. She opens the car door, walks up the path, ascends the front steps, and rings the doorbell. After waiting a minute or so, she rings again. Kristen then about-faces and begins to march back down the path, stopping to peer into the window. What does she see? She shrugs, returns to her car, and leaves.

As tempted as I am to ask her to explain herself this instant, I elect instead to let her explain later. The last scene records our visit to the house. It's interesting to watch Ken's facial expressions. He's good, he's very good. I can still hear his fake stutter.

Sarah breaks the silence in the room. "There were a number of other visits from Ken, almost daily, in fact. I think we haven't heard much from Kristen, and now would be a good time." So much for subtleties.

"I was simply curious. Getting a call from Robert to take over and run a company where the three principals had disappeared was a little weird. So I simply went to the house to look." Plausible.

"Just so you know, from the time you first appeared at GSS, you have been under surveillance, not only by us, but by Fitzgerald's people as well, and possibly by one of Robert's agents," Sarah says. "We're convinced that you are who you say you are, and that going to their house was simply an act of curiosity."

Sighing, I glance at my watch. It's almost seven o'clock. No wonder I'm getting hungry again. "I have several immediate concerns. Our safety for one, and secondly, if Kristen's house is under observation, by whomever, how does she get back in?" I hope I'm being calm, under the circumstances.

"You and Kristen left her house about fifteen minutes ago in your car and are going out to dinner here in the North End...again." Sarah is cold as ice. "That will make the transition easy. I think it would be best for you two to stay another night together at Kristen's house. That way, it will be assumed that you've been temporarily distracted. Tomorrow, you'll call Ed Harris and tell him that you tried to call him several times and were under the weather. He'll know that you spent the day and night with Kristen, smile briefly at your deceit, and call Mr. Galjarian. You'll be expected in his office at ten. Then the hard part begins: trying to lay a trap for Fitzgerald and those working with him, while not exposing anyone to excessive risk."

"What about Mays? What's his role?" Frankly, this FBI connection gives me the creeps.

"Deputy Director Mays has come to depend on Fitzgerald for almost everything, and it was in Fitzgerald's interest to be the perfect executive assistant. Mays has no chance of becoming director, and his rise to deputy and tenure has been a combination of his personal hard work, good luck on several big cases, and the fact that Fitzgerald has been helping him for over ten years. The problem lies in the fact that despite his years of dedicated service, Fitzgerald is the leader of a rogue element within the Bureau, protected by his position with Mays, who looks the other way because of his misplaced loyalty."

I scratch my head. "Rogue element. I really don't understand."

"Fitzgerald believes that the country has gotten soft and that 9/11 was the tip of the iceberg. He has choreographed at least a dozen suicide-appearing deaths and has advocated that the FBI's powers extend to overseas anti-terrorism, including assassinations and otherwise assisting in the overthrow of governments he thinks are anti-American." Sarah draws a deep breath. "He is a very dangerous man.

"While we were initially unsure where the threat was originating, we knew it was internal and that Fitzgerald was planning to get the Ebola and presumably an antidote, and launch his own private army of followers. In addition to being dangerous, he's very forceful and has recruited at least a dozen men and women whom we've been able to identify."

I want to pinch myself and wake up from this nightmare. How are we supposed to ferret out a senior FBI agent and his recruits, protected unwittingly by the deputy director? And how are we going to convince anybody? Well, the tapes certainly help. But still, I keep thinking of the danger factor, now that the case for which I was hired has been solved.

"I think that Kristen should be removed from the equation." I do my best to sound assertive. "There's too much risk."

"So long as the element of surprise is on our side," Jacob says, "the danger factor is reduced. Nobody is giving Kristen any real attention. They're beginning to take notice of you, but since Fitzgerald has heard every word you've ever spoken to the deputy director, he's comfortable that you're off on a wild goose chase and pose no threat. No, we've got to bait a trap and close it tight, and quickly."

"What about picking up Ken or someone else you've identified, and getting him to confess?" Kristen's voice sounds unnaturally high.

"Shall we use torture? No, Kristen, we need to set a trap that will catch all the vermin at the same time."

"Do you have such a trap?"

"Depending on Robert, we might," Sarah remarks.

I'm confused. "But I thought you didn't trust Robert either."

"We don't, but I think he can be positioned to make this work. No one knows me, so I can be the messenger everyone has been waiting for, the one with the demands delivered to both Galjarian and Mays...through you, Stephen."

Oh shit!

"Tomorrow, as you're leaving Kristen's house for your meeting, you'll be kidnapped by two men wearing ski masks and taken to an undisclosed safe spot. You'll be given a list of demands to present, and to insure that you comply, Kristen will also be kidnapped and held at that same location until the demands are met."

I must have turned white as a sheet, because Ted rushes over with another glass of wine.

"Don't worry, Sarah's got it all figured out," he says.

Why am I not reassured?"

"Lazlo and Jacob will be your kidnappers; I'll kidnap Kristen. You'll both be brought here," Sarah says.

"Make sure that you pack whatever you'll need for a few days." Ted uncrosses his legs. "The guest rooms upstairs are very comfortable, and just let me know if there is anything special you like to eat or drink." He wants this to be a five-star abduction. "You'd better go now. You have reservations at Piani's on Hanover Street, near the expressway. Needless to say, the food is wonderful... southern. Your car is parked in the garage across from the Boston Garden. Second floor near the elevator. Jacob will show you out."

I turn to Kristen. "You okay?"

Her eyes are moist. "I'll be fine. I'm just a little scared."

Sarah walks across the room and gently places an arm

around Kristen. "It's the only way."

Maybe that satisfies Kristen, but it sure as hell doesn't make me feel all warm and fuzzy. These guys are all pros. Why do they need us?

Jacob awakens me from my thoughts. "We have to go out the back into the alley. Just walk down about twenty feet, take a left, then a right onto Hanover. And…have a pleasant evening."

My sense of humor isn't really up to par, but another meal with Kristen in a cozy Italian restaurant the evening before we are kidnapped sounds almost…Shit, this whole thing sounds terrible. I vacillate between angry and scared, leaning heavily towards scared.

CHAPTER TWENTY-SEVEN

Entering Piani helps my attitude immeasurably. Pasta, pasta, and more pasta. It is the essence of what comforts the soul. Bucatini, tagliatelle, fusilli, rigatoni, vermicelli, and spaghetti.

The walls and tables are covered with tiles, reflecting the bright spirit of Campania. From Mount Vesuvius to Amalfi to Naples, the dominant gastronomic feature of Italy takes on a whole new meaning.

I can't express the relief I feel that the kidnapping isn't scheduled until tomorrow. I peek furtively at Kristen. Her eyes are still heavy and downcast, although I sense she is trying to rally for my sake. Chianti and spaghetti with the house meat sauce is the ideal antidote for the blahs. Well, not blahs exactly, more like the creepies. What have I gotten us into? Why does this seem like The Last Supper?

Without saying a word, we are whisked away by the hostess and seated in the back of the restaurant, which is deceptively larger than it appears from the street. I'm beginning to feel as though we're part of the cast of one of those stereotypical movies about the mob. A wicker-wrapped bottle of what I assume is Chianti suddenly appears, together with two glasses.

The last time I drank wine from a straw-covered bottle was in college, and I recall that it made a better candleholder than a drink.

I reconnoiter the room and since I don't see any wait staff, I decide to pour a small portion into my glass for tasting. Kristen tries to smile. Her attempt is really half-hearted. I swirl the dark red contents around the glass and steady myself for a frontal assault on my palate.

Stephen, you continually surpass yourself on the idiot scale. How many times have you said never judge a book by its cover? The wine rates somewhere between great and out of this world. It's definitely not the same stuff I drank in college.

I fill Kristen's glass. She reminds me of a baby bird who has just been pushed out of the nest. You'd better start flapping those wings before you hit the ground. She finally manages a smile. I fill my glass and raise it to hers. We each take a sip. Kristen grasps my free hand. Her skin is cold to the touch.

"Stephen, I'm not up to this. I just can't. Please tell them I can't." A tear forms in the corner of her eye.

I bring her hand to my lips and give her fingertips a kiss. "Let's eat, and at least for a few moments we can pretend we're gazing out at Capri."

Kristen again feigns a smile. It is decidedly sad that no candles adorn our table. Maybe the fire inspector is expected to pay a visit soon and the candles are being hidden until his departure. We've got to get out of this gloom-and-doom mood.

An older man approaches our table. I feel my body

grow tense. He passes us, gives us a toothless grin, and proceeds down a hall. If I had been more observant and less self-absorbed, I would have noticed the men's room sign pointing down the hall. Why am I so high-strung? Because I'm scared shitless.

Our waiter appears and hands us menus, then turns and quickly walks away. Far different from the other night, when I thought the waiter was going to join us for dinner. Maybe good waiters get vibes from their guests and react accordingly. These people want to engage, and these people want to be left alone.

We simultaneously open our menus. Everything is in Italian, except the prices. Fortunately, the menu is simple and spectacular. I hope Kristen has an appetite. I do. No surprise.

Pasta con le Sarde (that's easy...sardines), *Ravioli di Barbabietole* (that's not so easy), *Cappelletti in Brodo* (getting harder)...*Spaghetti alla Carbonara* (that's the one).

"I thought I knew enough *cooking* Italian to eat in any restaurant in the world." Kristen's smile is now warmer and more relaxed. "I haven't even left Boston, and I recognize only about half of the dishes on this menu. But that half looks terrific, starting with *Pasta con la Norma*."

I raise an eyebrow high enough that Kristen immediately adds, "Penne with eggplant and basil."

"And the *Spaghetti alle Vongole*," I say.

"I wonder...are clams like oysters, best eaten in months ending with the letter *r*?" Kristen seems to regain some enthusiasm.

Not only does she tell me that she knows what I plan to order, but her culinary knowledge extends into an area of deep personal concern to me — oysters, which I will save for another time.

I look up to find our waiter ready for our order. We

speak, he listens, he nods, he leaves.

Unlike a lot of restaurants, especially Italian restaurants, the music here is thankfully not directed toward the elevator sounds of Monteverde meeting Dean Martin. We are treated to traditional light classical music which mingles with the voices of the patrons, most of whom are conversing in Italian, a good sign. Another great North End discovery.

We speak little throughout dinner, in part because the food is great, and in part because neither of us knows what to say to the other, except to acknowledge that we have targets painted on our backs saying *kidnap me*.

I think Kristen senses that I can't protect her from whatever is going down, and that our survival depends on people we don't even know. Why the hell shouldn't we simply walk away? The simple answer is that we're already in too deep, and we aren't really secure until this gang of nuts is put away. Which gang of nuts is it? Lazlo, Jacob, sister Sarah, and Ted, or Fitzgerald and the FBI renegades, or Robert and whoever is aligned with him? Shit, this whole thing is pretty damned dangerous and is way too complicated.

I empty the wine basket. It's now after nine, and I signal our waiter to bring the check. He shakes his head. This entire evening is becoming more and more like a movie. I gesture again for the check. The waiter shrugs and walks away. I guess our kidnapping hosts have taken care of that detail, too. I leave a twenty-dollar bill as a tip, although the total elapsed time we were waited upon was less than a minute. Wow, that's six hundred dollars per hour. I don't know any lawyers who charge that much.

I help Kristen with her coat, and we head toward the door. She links her arm in mine and gives it a squeeze. I lean over and give her a quick kiss on the cheek. No one in the restaurant even looks or cares.

The air is chilly, and the wind stings my face. I am

totally exhausted. I'm surprised I can even stand. What if I sleep through the kidnapping? Kristen snuggles close to me, and I try to block the wind from her. She seems frail. I guess they don't teach this at business school or law school.

We walk from the North End, past the old Boston Garden toward the North Station garage, where my car is parked, hopefully. It's dark and cold and altogether not the place of my dreams. I'm glad the formerly elevated portion of the Green Line subway is now underground. Its massive steel structure would have blocked what little light there is.

Kristen and I enter the garage and immediately decide to walk the reasonably well-lighted stairs to the second floor rather than wait for an elevator, which might not come and might be housing a homeless person or two on this cold night. I keep thinking about the billions of dollars that have been sunk into bailouts, while people are on the street simply unable to feed and shelter themselves. So much for politics.

We climb the stairs as quickly as possible. Why chance fate? When we open the door to the second floor, to my surprise and great relief, I spot my faithful Volvo. I dig out my keys and walk, with increasing speed, to the car. Kristen is keeping pace, and I sense that she is relieved that we are going back to Cambridge. I walk around to the passenger door, insert the key, and with a gesture reminiscent of Sir Walter Raleigh, beckon my lady to enter.

Suddenly my arms are pinned behind my back. I look up and see another pair of hands grabbing Kristen. Christ! I was so damned relieved to see the car, I forgot to look around. Shit! Kristen lets out a sharp shriek, which is instantly muffled by a gloved hand. Whoever is holding my arms knows exactly what he is doing. The pain is sharp enough for me to know not to try anything stupid. I stop resisting and try to normalize my breathing. In through the nose — out through the mouth. It would be pretty stupid to pass out for lack of oxygen. My captor loosens his grip, ever so slightly. I see four people, each of whom is wearing a black ski mask. A million thoughts crash through my mind. Is this a preview of tomorrow's kidnapping, a run-through? Or has the timetable been somehow moved forward? Or…

Before I can even open my big mouth to speak, one of my captors slaps a piece of duct tape over my mouth. He turns and does the same to Kristen. Our hands are then each taped together.

I am roughly spun around and find myself face to face with a large automatic weapon. Is all this really necessary? Is this a dress rehearsal, or have we entered the FBI's equivalent of the *Twilight Zone*?

"We don't want to kill you, but we will if it becomes necessary."

"Jesus, Mary, and Joseph," I mutter to myself. The voice that utters the threat is not the voice of Jacob or Sarah Kettleman, Lazlo Onellon or Ted Gordon, but that of none other than rogue Special Agent Jack Fitzgerald. I am about to cry or possibly wet my pants. Everything is going wrong.

Kristen's eyes reflect terror the likes of which I have never seen before. I try to fight back tears, which is hard if you can't rub your eyes. I look at our three other captors. All are dressed in black from head to toe, each wearing a black ski mask. I wonder whether a black ski mask is standard issue for kidnappers. Remember, in through the nose and out through the mouth. Shit! My mouth is taped. And how the hell did Fitzgerald learn of the staged kidnapping plans? And why here in the garage?

I see only one weapon. I guess Fitzgerald wasn't worried about excessive firepower from me. We aren't exactly in a position to put up much of a struggle. This sucks! If they know about the real-fake kidnapping, they probably know about the secret hideout. Wait a minute, why am I assuming they know anything? Fitzgerald may simply want to kidnap us for ransom or possibly interrogate us to see what we know. Sarah was so sure that they had written Kristen off and already knew what I knew. So why us and why now? I'm getting myself more, rather than less confused. Did they follow us here from the North End?

Fitzgerald herds us toward the stairs. Two of the kidnappers quickly ascend to the floor above.

I hear a muffled *okay* from the staircase. We are half-led and half-pushed up the stairs. Fitzgerald partially opens the door. He assumes a crouching position. I catch a glance at the two advance men looking around the almost-empty parking garage. This is not a good place for us to be in. Fitzgerald rises and opens the door fully and strides out. The two kidnappers who had preceded us stop and turn toward Fitzgerald.

The noise is deafening. At least ten rounds of automatic pistol fire ravage Fitzgerald's body. His gun falls to the concrete only a microsecond before he, or what's left of him, does. I see the fourth captor freeze, and then slowly fall backward down the stairs. A red spot spreads across the back of his black suit.

Kristen is so pale, I'm certain she's in shock. I don't feel so good myself. That's an understatement. Maybe I shouldn't have eaten so much pasta. I walk directly toward the gun-toting assailants, trying to get between them and Kristen, who is going to crumble any second. I am either being very brave or very stupid. The hooded pair lower their weapons and remove their hoods.

Goddammit. Jacob Kettleman and Robert Galjarian. Son of a bitch. We've been set up since the beginning. I feel used — dirty. We've been the lure, while Fitzgerald, or what's left of him, the trophy.

Simultaneously, I hear the squeal of tires and the sound of footsteps behind me. I quickly look over my shoulder and see Sarah, a man whom I don't recognize wearing a business suit, and another ski-masked man, presumably the shooter from below. Sarah has Kristen in her arms and is talking to her in calm tones, while the *suit* removes the tape from her hands and mouth. I look behind the door and see the two captors whom Kettleman and Galjarian had replaced lying still. Thankfully no pool of blood is spreading across the floor. I'm beginning to feel nauseated and I'm also the only one who still has bound hands and a taped mouth.

The tire squealing grows louder, and a silver Crown Victoria rocks to a stop. The tinted window slowly lowers, and do you think I'm surprised to see Deputy Director Mays peering out at me? You bet your ass I am, and more than a little pissed. Jacob steps over the still body of former Special Agent Fitzgerald and unceremoniously rips the duct tape from my mouth. Thank God I shaved off my moustache years ago. Needless to say, there are a lot of questions I want answered. Everything seems to be happening in slow motion. As my mouth opens, Jacob puts his hand to my lips, Galjarian raises his hand to signal silence, and the door of the deputy director's car opens. He emerges. I nod. I'll shut up, but only for a minute. The *suit* appears and removes the tape from my wrists. I see Kristen sobbing, uncontrollably, but silently, on Sarah's shoulder.

I am now facing the most unlikely threesome: Jacob Kettleman — employer unknown; Robert Galjarian — employer uncertain; and William Howard Mays — employer FBI; together with several dead bodies.

I raise my hand, third-grade like. "I'd really like to know what the hell just went down here. But first I need to go to the bathroom very badly, and then I need a drink. And I think Kristen does as well."

"Fine. Lazlo and Ted are back at our apartment, and have prepared some dessert and a myriad of liquid refreshments." Jacob is talking about going back for a nightcap as though we just left a movie theater. These guys are all crazy.

"Stephen," Robert Galjarian begins, "don't dwell on what just happened or you'll go nuts."

Go nuts! Now there's a thought. Let's see, I am angry, confused, and really have to go to the bathroom.

Sarah walks Kristen through the door, and although her eyes are red, she seems to have pulled herself together. Thank God, since I know I'm going to fall apart, it's only a matter of where and when, but I want some answers first.

Several men in fatigues arrive to clean up the mess. I notice that one of Fitzgerald's men is being helped to his feet, cuffed with what looks like a large tie wrap, and escorted toward a Chevy Suburban which has pulled up behind Mays' car. I didn't even see it arrive.

"Please get into my car." I suddenly notice that Deputy Director Mays is standing with only the aid of a cane. No leg braces.

He sees that I am staring. "Things aren't always what they seem," he says.

"I'll make sure your car is brought around," Jacob offers.

I reach into my coat pocket and hand him my keys. I feel and undoubtedly look like shit, but at least we're alive, the bad guys are dead, the scientists have been found, and the spread of the plague has been averted. All in less than a week. I think I deserve a bonus! A big bonus.

I start trembling even before Mays' car reaches the ground level of the parking garage. At first I shiver, then start to shake. My heart is pumping at least twice as fast as normal, and likely twice as loud. I'm having trouble catching my breath. I've just seen a man's body torn apart by a barrage of bullets, albeit he was trying to kidnap us at the time. A second man was killed as well.

Let's revisit what just...happened. We were used as bait to destroy a dangerous animal, threatened, bound and gagged, lied to and generally abused. In retrospect, I didn't save the world, because it wasn't really in danger. I just didn't know that minor fact. And what about Ed and Henry? Are they part of this? What is *this*, anyway? A plot? A conspiracy? A joint enterprise between intelligence agencies? Legal or extra-legal?

The Crown Victoria pulls up in front of the scientists' North End hideaway. Since there is never a space in the North End, we double park. I'd give anything to see one of Boston's finest tow Mays' car.

The driver opens the door for the deputy director, whose presence I hadn't registered since leaving the garage. He climbs out of the car with surprising grace, using his cane as a prop as much as an aid.

Kristen and I slowly slide across the seat. I'm barely able to stand, although my pulse has slowed significantly. Kristen peers up at me. Her eyes reveal so many emotions: fear, confusion, anger, and something else...relief, or is she happy to be with me? What a time to ask dumb questions.

CHAPTER TWENTY-EIGHT

Ted buzzes us upstairs and greets us.

"No arguments," he says. "I want each of you to go directly to the third floor. There are two guest bathrooms. We took the liberty of bringing over some clean clothes and personal toiletries. Take a long, hot shower. Trust me, you'll feel a lot better."

Kristen and I exchange glances. It's hard to argue with Ted's logic, and the idea of hot water pelting down on me is very appealing. On second thought, I'd rather take a quick shower and a long bath with Kristen. I have a great imagination.

The third floor is finished comparably in quality to the second. The bathrooms are located at opposite ends of the hall. I decide that Kristen should have first choice.

"If we had more time, you could wash my back and I'd wash yours." Kristen smiles and closes the door of the nearest bathroom. My pulse starts going crazy again. I drag myself to the far end of the hall.

This is my week for great bathrooms: two sinks — check; lighting that makes it easy to shave — check; marble walls and floor — check; with heated floors — double check; and with multiple showerheads so that all of you gets rinsed at the same time — check again.

Don't forget big, fluffy terry towels — big check.

I hate to admit it, but Ted was right. After a shave and a shower, I feel 100 percent better. Not only did I wash off the dirt of the day, but also the kind of dirt that was clinging to me after this evening's events, dirt by association. I do feel better and cleaner.

I glance down the hall toward Kristen's bathroom. The door is open. Should I peek in? Tacky. But I do it anyway. I guess she got herself together faster than I.

I stand at the top of the stairs and stare at the floor below. It looks like an intimate Saturday evening cocktail party, not a post-mortem. Everyone seems to have found the time to change into appropriate attire. I look over the crowd before descending. All the players are here, except Ed Harris and Henry Barnett. Curious. Even some folks I don't know. There is something very disturbing about the scene. I join the gathering.

Robert Galjarian rushes over to greet me. "What would you like to drink? I know we have a bit of explaining to do, but you definitely need a drink first."

"A Negroni on the rocks if possible." I need something strong. Maybe I'll be able to control my temper if I have a couple of drinks. Maybe not. In any event, I'm sure his answers will not satisfy me. Pretty negative, but not without reason.

Ted, whose ears seem to simultaneously tune into several channels at once, appears with my Negroni: a concoction of gin, Campari, and sweet vermouth — two cubes and a lemon peel. It tastes like cough medicine. An acquired taste, but soothing on the back of the throat after a hard day at the office.

"We've taken the liberty of asking Ed and Henry to join us." I'm relieved to see that Colonel Galjarian is looking a bit rumpled himself. "It'll be a few minutes before they get here, since neither had any advance notice of tonight's activities." Does this mean that Ed and Henry are good guys or simply out of the loop? More questions and no answers.

I give Robert a perfunctory nod and seek out Kristen. She looks fabulous, considering that she was dressed in silver duct tape less than half an hour ago. She is deeply engaged in a discussion with Mays and a beautiful young African-American woman.

"Stephen!" The deputy director may have found his legs, and he hasn't lost his voice. "I would like you to meet my daughter, Julia. She's attending the Kennedy School of Government."

Julia extends her hand. "I've heard so much about you from Dad." She gives her father a smile. I pinch myself to make sure I'm not having a macabre dream.

"Julia was a member of the US Olympic women's crew team." Mays beams with pride.

Kristen and I exchange glances. People have just died, and we're making small talk with one of the participants.

"May I borrow your father?" I ask.

"Only for a minute," Julia says. I wonder if she is clueless or has been briefed, or has she developed a certain immunity after years of exposure to her father's line of work?

Mays gives his daughter a quick kiss. "Be right back."

As soon as we're a couple of steps away from Kristen and Julia, I ask, "What the hell is going on?"

"As soon as Ed and Henry arrive. Be patient for a few more minutes."

"Patience, patience, my ass. You and your merry bunch of madmen almost got us killed tonight." I am using every bit of self-control to prevent myself from starting to scream.

"A few more minutes." He pats my arm and rejoins his daughter.

I've gotten myself involved with a bunch of lunatics. Dangerous lunatics. Does he think patting my arm is going to calm me down?

Kristen excuses herself from a number of people who have joined Julia and the deputy director, and heads toward me. I take a deep gulp of my Negroni.

Kristen's shower seems to have lifted her spirits. The terror of the last hour has been rinsed away — at least superficially. "Has anyone said anything of substance to you yet?" Her voice has a sharp edge to it.

"Nothing at all. Mays told me to be patient. Wait for Ed and Henry to arrive."

"This is bullshit."

Kristen is really pissed off.

"There's dessert in the kitchen...buffet-style," Ted announces. This guy is something else. I'm sure he must think about things other than food, but when? I can relate.

"Interested?" I ask Kristen.

"Not just yet. I'm going to circulate. See if I can get some insight."

"Okay. I'll see you in a sec." I move toward the food.

The drink is beginning to settle in my stomach. I'm not feeling any pain, but I know it's inevitable. Believe it or not, I think I'll pass on dessert, but to be polite, I should at least see what's out there — and Ed and Henry aren't going to arrive for a few more minutes.

I'm uncomfortable with the fact that I am attending a party while Fitzgerald's body isn't even cold yet, but the sight of the Ted Gordon look-alike sitting in the front seat of the Range Rover with part of his head missing and acts of terrorism being conducted in the name of America, is enough to help me overcome this temporary sense of guilt. I head toward the kitchen.

This group must have been supremely confident in tonight's outcome. This party has a certain air of planning to it.

Ted has prepared a dessert table adorned with floral arrangements featuring bittersweet, lavender, and eucalyptus. The smell is heavenly and equal only to the food, which includes several homemade pies — apple, pumpkin, and my favorite, strawberry-rhubarb; the richest-looking vanilla ice cream I've ever seen; enough cheese and crackers, fresh pears, and apples for a small army, which I guess accurately describes the *guest list*; and a selection of white wines from France, Spain, and Germany. Martha Stewart, eat your heart out.

I decide to postpone indulging until after the debriefing has been completed, if I can stay awake that long and if I'm satisfied with the explanation that I hope will be forthcoming. On second thought, maybe I had better get just one small piece of pie now. I stroll toward the front of the living room. The evening is beginning to catch up with me. Even my bones are beginning to ache. Kristen excuses herself from another group and crosses over to me.

I'm debating giving her a big hug and kiss, when Ed Harris and Henry Barnett are ushered into the room.

There are no words to describe their faces, as they stare first at Lazlo, then Jacob, and lastly Ted. You'd think they were being confronted by the ghost of Christmas Past, which in the case of Ted makes sense. Before either can speak, Ted rushes over, not to take a drink order, but to prevent poor Henry, who has just locked eyes on William Howard Mays, from having a heart attack.

Robert Galjarian seems to be taking charge. He asks everyone to be quiet, find a seat, and listen to what he promises will be a short speech.

"Tonight, an historic two-year combined effort between military and civilian agencies, together with several concerned citizens, has resulted in the destruction of the most dangerous kind of terrorist cell — one of our own. Everyone here has been involved in the success of this enterprise. In some instances…" he pauses and focuses upon Kristen and me, "…you may not have known the degree of your personal involvement."

No shit!

Kristen grabs my hand in hers and gives it a hard squeeze. I think she senses that I'm about to beat Robert Galjarian over the head with the deputy director's cane.

"Agent Fitzgerald crossed the line from being a soldier in the war against terrorism to being a terrorist. He believed he was above the law of man. He was on his own Jihad, his own holy war to eradicate those he perceived to be America's enemy. He was prepared to do anything necessary to fullfill his mission, even kill. Before we could cut off the head of the snake, it was absolutely essential that we ferret out those with whom he had allied himself and those who had allied themselves to him."

I am beginning to feel nauseated.

"No larger a group than minimally necessary could know what was going on. Remember, the man was an insider and had access to a lot of resources. Everyone had to play a role, and those roles had to be credible, which is easiest to accomplish if the actor's performance is genuine."

Again he gazes at Kristen and me. Several others are looking at us and nodding.

"Courage is often overrated, since it's usually only

an instinctive response to an event. You know...*it seemed like a good idea at the time*. However, pursuing the truth without wavering is the measure of greatness, and we are in your debt. America's in your debt."

This guy is good. All I need is a little flag to wave. That's not fair. These people have spent a whole lifetime being patriots. I only did it for less than a week. It's hard to stay angry after a speech like that.

"Fitzgerald theorized," he continues, "that if he could control GSS's research and key personnel, he could prevent it from falling into the hands of the enemy. Of course, he turned out to be the enemy. Had he not been stopped, the world faced a crisis of biblical proportions. Nothing justifies using innocent people, without their consent, to achieve our goal, but I hope I've at least in some small way explained it."

I turn toward Kristen and shrug. She nods. I take an- other sip of my drink. The room is dead quiet. Believe it or not, I've got nothing to say. I'm still not happy, but I'm moderately satisfied with our role in the events as they unfolded. I still don't like being used. That reminds me, I've got a bill to prepare.

Slowly, people begin to move around and talk. Does that mean I can get dessert? I start to lead Kristen toward the kitchen.

"I want to say something. Please, everyone, listen up," Ed Harris shouts. Again everyone stops talking. He clasps his hands behind his back and starts to pace. He looks like George C. Scott in the opening scene of *Patton*.

"I've been a first-class coward. I am grateful that I've been pretty much kept in the dark since I probably would have had a heart attack if I had any idea of what was going on." The audience responds with an uncomfortable murmur of agreement. "Instead of rolling up my sleeves and finding out what was happening, I dragged a friend into a potentially deadly situation. For what? Because I didn't have the guts. Well, there is something I can do, and I am sure that Henry will back me up."

By the look on Henry Barnett's face, it's clear that he has no idea what's going on.

"The work that GSS is doing is truly remarkable and presents immeasurable opportunities. Eradication of dis- ease, or at least successful treatment, has been the goal of caring people since the beginning of time. The advances that have been made will make everyone associated with GSS very wealthy.

"Capital Investments will be setting up a charitable foundation which it will initially fund with 10 million dollars, adding 10 percent of our company profits each year." Ed stops to gauge the reaction of the crowd.

"The money will be used to encourage children in the pursuit of their dreams, whether in the arts, journalism, science, sports...whatever. And Kristen, I would like you to be the first president of the foundation."

The man is on a roll. Kristen starts to breathe rapidly.

"Stephen," he continues, "you've had to endure a lot of shit because of me, pardon my French..."

I thought it was *merde* in French.

"...but you came when I called, and jumped into a mess of gigantic proportions, never hesitating to move forward. Most people would have walked away. I am asking the board of GSS, who happen to be assembled here, to issue you stock equal to 10 percent of the authorized shares, and a seat on the board."

I'm getting dizzy. Wait! Does this mean he doesn't expect a bill?

"Hear, hear..." Ted, Lazlo, Jacob, Sarah, and Robert shout in unison, joined by Henry, who seems to have caught up with the flow. I gaze toward the back of the room and am having a hard time focusing. I think Ted is moving toward the kitchen again. Yes, and he returns with four bottles of champagne.

Glasses appear, and the conversation returns to small talk. I feel like I've just ridden the world's largest and scariest roller coaster, but I didn't fall out, so it's okay, right?

Ed approaches me and he places his hand on my shoulder.

"Just between you and me..."

I can't take too much more rah-rah.

"...this has been the best wakeup call I could ever have had. Quality and quantity had become one and the same, and that's wrong." A tear falls from his eye. "I've never been so frightened and had so little control."

I understand his feelings. When you're a strong and bright person like Ed and find yourself being swept away in a current over which you have no power, it's a bad time all around.

"I understand." I hope I sound reassuring.

All of a sudden, Henry appears, recovered from the initial revelations of this evening. "Stephen," he begins, "despite what the board voted, you can't eat stock in a privately held corporation. I expect you to personally hand-deliver your bill for services, which, based on the time expended..."

Oh shit! Henry's going to nickel-and-dime me on my bill.

"...I calculate to be $50,000. Cheap, if you ask me." He is chuckling to himself. I guess he's tripled my hourly rate based on performance. I'm okay with that.

Jacob joins us. "We've decided to hold a board meeting tomorrow morning at eight o'clock at the offices." He says to Kristen. "We would like you to attend. You've been the caretaker, and we'll need a status report."

We both look as though we've been shot through the heart. I wanted to sleep in tomorrow, preferably with Kristen. Jacob starts laughing, not a little laugh, but a guffaw. I had, until this point, yet to see him even as much as smile. "Just a joke."

I let out a sigh and catch a grin on Kristen's face.

"We won't be starting 'til noon."

Now he's serious.

"Good night, everyone," I say, clutching Kristen's hand. "Sorry to miss dessert. I really am. But it has been a tough day for us and…"

Deputy Director Mays' voice booms, "A car is waiting downstairs to take you both to Cambridge. Your Volvo has been returned to Kristen's driveway."

"Until tomorrow." Jacob is still relishing his dumb joke.

"Tomorrow and tomorrow and tomorrow creeps in this petty pace…"

Also by D.G. Stern

There's Always Tomorrow A Chris Callahan Mystery

For younger readers:
The Loneliest Tree

25 Days Of A Tropical Christmas

Upton Charles - Dog Detective:
Disappearing Diamonds
Something Fishy
Winter Wonderland
Lost Loot

Non-fiction:
GOLF a la CARTE-Volume One

NEPTUNE PRESS

WWW.NEPTUNEPRESS.ORG